THE KNIGHT IN THE PANTHER SKIN
BOOK ONE OF THE TRILOGY

AVTANDIL'S QUEST

AN ADAPTATION OF SHOTA RUSTAVELI'S EPIC
12th CENTURY GEORGIAN POEM

WRITTEN BY
H. J. BUELL & ANA GABUNIA
https://hjbuell.com

COPYRIGHT AND PRINTING

<u>ACKNOWLEDGEMENTS</u>

ARTWORK

- Irakli Kakhadze, Cover Artwork
- Dasha Massalskaya, Layout and Design

CONTENT EDITORS

- Michael Arizola, Rose Marie (Peggy) Parris

DEVELOPMENTAL EDITORS

- Zobaid Alam
- Luka Bandzeladze
- Chrissy Buell
- Benjamin Kastin
- Alexander Edward Loughead
- Dane S. Muckler PhD
- Marek Suliga, Khatia Turmanidze
- Edward Wilson

MUSIC AND AUDIOBOOK

- David (Dato) Toradze and Company

SPECIAL ACKNOWLEDGEMENTS

- Julie Cheung, Ali Farhad Howaida, John Jeys, Rishi Lakhani, Tina Mamulashvili, Sea Dog, The Rat, and Marjorie Wardrop
- Mokvare Guest House: https://mokvare.ge
- Red and Tan Nation: https://redandtannation.com

<u>**DEDICATION**</u>

Avtandil's Quest is written out of respect for Georgia, home of the Caucasus Mountains and a people unlike any other in the world.
Most importantly, this work is dedicated to my wife Ana. Without her support, devotion to family, and observance of the original poem's traditions, this book would not have been possible.

Sweetheart, I love you. I will carry your burden.
Sakvarelo, Mikvarkhar. Genacvale.

Georgian Soul
H. J. Buell

The day's last sun has long since set
We count each star, our lips unmet
By the palest light, we make wine
I and this Georgian girl of mine

Lost in endless mountains and sky
I know I'm home, but can't say why
My heart blooms, though I dare not ask
How love ensnared my soul so fast

Nowhere else have I felt so much
I'm afraid, though we've yet to touch
I'd try to run, for it's too soon
Yet I'm caught by this Georgian moon

Sakvarelo, as she draws near
Mikvarkhar, whispered in my ear
Genacvale, here I will stay
Where I found love a poet's way

A FEW WORDS ON THE ORIGINAL

This book is a faithful adaptation of the original Knight in the Panther Skin, composed by Shota Rustaveli in 12th century Georgia. Although little is known about him, the poem's prologue indicates it was written to praise the first female ruler of Georgia - Tamar Mepe (King Tamar). Some historians believe he was in love with her, as his writings allude to this. But, like all great works, the original is not without controversy or debate. To this day, his writing is a pillar of Georgian culture. It stands alone as the most significant literary accomplishment of Georgia. The original poem is written in Rustavelian Quatrains, consisting of four sixteen syllable rhyming lines. In total, the poem comprises 1,662 of these, totaling 6,648 lines. To this day, some can recite the entire verse from memory and do so each year at annual events.

　　We've done our best to accurately capture the spirit and meaning of the story. However, cultural, and linguistic barriers limit the ability of anyone to fully express the true beauty of this text in anything other than its original Georgian form. What you read in this book is an honest adaptation of Shota's poem as an English literary novel.

　　Hopefully, after reading the story, you'll want to experience Georgia for yourself. Perhaps you might even try learning the language. For additional resources, comments, and information about the country and traditions, please visit our website.

https://hjbuell.com

TABLE OF CONTENTS

INTRODUCTION

AN UNEXPECTED MEETING

There are areas of the world lost to time where a particular magic comes to life. Some say these places exist between the Renaissance of Europe and the Empir e of Rome. Others claim to have found them in the ruins of far older civilizations or outlined in handprints on cave walls and carved into petroglyphs. Much like sunsets, their beauty is undeniable, yet the experience is different for everyone.

For me, I found one such place in an old wine bar, somewhere between the first and last cups of a brilliant burgundy red. It was there I met a man named Ilia. He was old, with a face etched like the bricks of the cellar we drank in.

How long he sat and talked with me is lost, but the story he told pulled me out of place and time. Eventually I lost track of where or even when I sat, but I remember why, and the why of a story is often more important than any other part. This was no exception.

He recited an ancient tale, orally passed from one person to the next for almost a thousand years. As I came to learn, it was first told by a man who loved a woman and his nation, yet neither could acknowledge him. Therein lies the first thread of this tragedy. His story is faithfully retold here, but to truly experience it, you might want to sit down with a glass of Kvarelian red.

CHAPTER 01

THE STORY OF ROSTEVAN

Storms forever darkened the horizons of men, but some people did not fear the unrest these times brought. To them, the darkness was no more than angry clouds hiding skies of azure crowned with gold. They knew misfortune often lingered on the winds of Fate, and the rule of Kings ebbed and flowed across generations like the tides of an endless sea.

One such man held lordship over the vast Kingdom of Arabia, commanding a host of near countless Knights. Rostevan was his name, and none were his equal in battle. His enemies feared the might of his armies, but the people loved him. He was wise, gracious, and fluent in speech. Yet today, despite his strength, he was unable to find peace.

A problem unlike any he faced in the past weighed on him, and he worried it might undo his entire Kingdom if left unresolved. Where commoners were free to worry and fret over their daily concerns, he had no such liberty. His duty bound him to lead his people into the coming sun, but the veil clouding his vision blinded him. For the first time in his rule, he could not decide what to do.

As he wrestled with his thoughts, his eyes roamed past the assembled courtiers and to the gardens. There, his daughter Tinatin, the joy and light of his life, stood next to a crystal fountain. She was his only child and had grown into a young woman without equal. All who laid eyes on her lost their hearts and minds. Many praised her, though only a poet's tongue could compose words worthy of her grace and beauty.

She smiled and waved when she saw her father, but he did not see her. His attention was once more on the matters before him, though his mind was elsewhere. The worry eating at him was a constant distraction. Seeing his daughter only deepened his concern. Though eager to speak in private with his chief advisor Sograt, he could not ignore the responsibilities of his Kingdom.

When at last the court retired, and he found himself alone, he called his advisors. For the wise always seek counsel before action. One by one, they arrived, seating themselves around him in a circle. Looking at the faces of men he had known and trusted for decades, he put his hands up in frustration.

"Friends, my mind is in turmoil, and I am unable to find relief. I cannot stop thinking about the future. A procession of Kings and Queens from the past consumes my thoughts. They march through my every waking moment but slip from my grasp before I can reach them. Like sands on the winds of time, they remind me of my own mortality."

"Their shadows grow long across me, and I fear my days in this world draw near to an end. Old age, most grievous of all ills, weighs upon me. If not today, then tomorrow I die. For this is the way of the world. Life is like the bud of a rose, which falls when dried and withered. Yet, what about our own futures?"

"When the sun sets on one of us, another flower must bloom in the garden, or we are all lost. You above all are aware I have no son to inherit my rule. Without an heir, the approach of this moonless night will consume us, for no joy exists in what darkness attends. In time, our Kingdom will fade into the pages of history and be gone forever. Knowing this, I have to act, but I do not know how to proceed."

"I have thought long on these things and would crown my daughter Tinatin as King, but she is not a man. I feared the people would not accept her, so I called you. With all your wisdom, what do you think of my idea? Give me your advice and help me find peace from this storm."

The Wisemen turned to one another, wordless, until Sograt spoke, gently admonishing his distraught King.

"You are wise to consider the future, but how can you talk of your age with us? We are all old here, and every living thing withers with time. Roses are no different. When one fades, the scent and color excel, and like you, they have no equal. Do not bury yourself so soon."

"These words are not flattery, but rather a light we hope to shine into the darkness weighing on your mind. Often, we have spoken of your daughter's deeds, which, like her radiance are revealed bright as the day. We advise you to appoint her as Regent. Allow no one to question your decision."

"She is a woman, but as Sovereign, she is begotten of God. Is it not true the children of lions are the same, whether they are male or female? She is no less a lion than you. When your time is finished, let her rule. Crown her and invite the people to celebrate, for they adore her."

Rostevan found peace in their words, shining like a fresh pearl. The fog clouding his mind dissipated, and his radiant face shone once more. He smiled, expressing his gratitude and devotion to his advisors.

"Your advice exceeds my grace, and the truth of your wisdom compels me to act. We will announce her as our future King!"

CHAPTER 02

A KING IS CROWNED

All courts and Kingdoms have secrets, yet few are kept. Arabia was no different. Before long, ladies and lords whispered Rostevan's plans between themselves until even commoners were discussing the coming event. Soon the news reached a particular young knight named Avtandil.

Tall and graceful as a cypress, his face was flawless, as if sculptured from marble. Of all the Knights, he was most favored among the people and loved as a son by the King. Though still beardless, he was a general of the armies, commanding hundreds of thousands of soldiers. Yet he carried a secret only he knew.

He was lovestruck by Tinatin. Every time he looked at her, the hosts of her obsidian eyelashes overcame his defenses. No matter what he did, the thorns of devotion pierced his heart, though he could not tell her. She was the jewel of the Kingdom and kept hidden.

Yet, the news of her coronation lit a fire in him. If appointed Regent, she would sit beside her father. His duties as general would invite him to gaze daily on her crystal face. He hoped seeing her more often might lead to a cure for his ailment, for he was slain with heartache. Such is the pity of love unspoken.

When the royal decree was announced, he read it with trembling hands.

"Hear me, for I am King Rostevan. One week from today,

I will appoint my daughter Tinatin as Regent. You are all invited to praise and extol her virtue. May her wisdom and grace illuminate us!"

The city's people were overjoyed at the announcement and spent the next seven days preparing to receive visitors. They set up banquet tables and hung flowers everywhere, welcoming guests until the castle and courtyards were overflowing. Everyone wanted to witness the first woman crowned as King.

One day before the event, servants brought the new throne to the square. The crowd gasped at its beauty. None had seen such craftsmanship. It was a work of art, wrought of gold and inlaid with pearls, rubies, emeralds, and sapphires. Yet it was a mere shadow compared to the King's daughter, for she had no equal. Jewels and riches were in every Kingdom, but one might find an angel feather before seeing another woman like her.

With the throne placed and only one day until her Regency, the citizens could not contain their excitement. People began celebrating in the streets as guests continued arriving from across the land. Some had even come from the distant borderlands beyond the frontier to pay their respects.

At the hour of the ceremony, everyone kneeled to give homage. Rostevan stood before his people, smiling as he raised his arms. He turned to Tinatin as she came out, radiant as the morning sun. Her rays kissed those gathered as though they were dew drops changed to diamonds by her gaze. Those who fell beneath her stare basked in the aura of her presence.

She walked towards her father with timid steps, smiling and waving to her people. He took her hands and seated her, removing his crown, and placing it on her head. The people shouted their approval as he handed her the scepter of rulership. By these acts, he showed her the devotion of a King. With the love of a father, he draped the royal robes around her shoulders.

Arms raised, he announced her as his heir. Everyone cheered as he bowed to his daughter. General Avtandil and his armies beat their shields, swearing allegiance to their new Regent. People blessed her and pronounced her as their Sovereign. They blew trumpets, clashing cymbals and ringing bells as they sang her praises throughout the city.

She turned from her throne and back to the people, and her heart filled with happiness. The praise and pride of her father lifted her spirits beyond her wildest dreams. His hand was the one she had been raised by, and now she was crowned by him.

Though full of joy, her thoughts unexpectedly turned to the day he would no longer be there to guide her. Overcome with emotion, she could not contain her sadness as she considered the meaning behind her Kingship. Silver tears glistened on her cheeks, drooping her eyelashes like the tail feathers of a raven. She could not imagine herself taking the throne from her father if it meant one day losing him. Yet, he understood and consoled her with words of wisdom.

"Do not weep, my daughter. Every father has a peer in his child. Until today I have not been able to extinguish the fires in my heart, for I worried no one would come after me to protect and shepherd our people. However, now you are our future King. From this day forward, our people are entrusted to your care. Be modest, discerning, and discreet in your actions."

"Never forget the sun shines alike on roses and dung heaps. Knowing this, do not grow weary in your mercy to classes and castes of people. With only your hand, you can bind the free, and they will obey. But to rule well, you cannot hoard wealth. Remember, you must spread the bounty of your Kingdom for prosperity to flow throughout the realm. For do the seas not also pour forth the floods they receive?"

"Be excessive in all you do to benefit our people, as generosity in Kings is like the aloe planted in Eden. All, including the traitor, are obedient to the generous. Everyone takes joy in eating and drinking, yet none profit from hoarding. What you give to your people is forever yours, while what you keep is lost. Be mindful of your responsibilities, and your people will always remember their duty to you."

Rostevan shared all these words and more with the young maiden. Though newly appointed as Regent, she listened to her father's advice, never growing weary of his instruction. When he finished speaking, they embraced. Her tears were gone, replaced with the resolve she would one day rule with.

She smiled as she watched her father leave to sport and

drink with his Knights and advisors. He was joyful as a young lion and filled with pride in her. Though happy for his joy, she did not join the celebration. The depth of Rostevan's wisdom had ignited a fire in her, and she summoned her servants.

"Bring me what I have been given over the years as the daughter of Arabia. Find every one of the jewels we have sealed away and place them before my throne."

All she owned was brought out, and she gave everything she had to the people. Those gathered for the coronation received gifts she cherished since childhood. Colorful gems and golden goblets were handed out like pastries until she gave away the last of her possessions. When there was nothing left, she called the Master of the Horse and issued orders to him.

"Now, I will do what my father taught me. Go, and open whatever treasure rooms we have! Lead in droves of asses, camels, horses, and mules. Bring the army to help you and take all you find to the square. Let the wealth of our Kingdom be distributed to her people. Do not keep back any part. Give to all and let none go without!"

Soldiers came and helped, emptying gilded vaults like pirates raiding ships. Treasures unlike any seen before or since were given away, yet her hands never tired of giving. There appeared to be no end to her generosity.

Jubilant youths rode away with her delicate and sleek Arab steeds. At the same time, silks and sculptures were carried away from the palace corners and walls by young men and women. Priceless paintings, baubles, and an endless stream of riches flowed into the hands of the populace. She showered wealth down on her people like a snowstorm. Not a youth or maiden went without.

Thus was the first day of Tinatin's rule. The people sang praises to her and loved her as no other King before. Their joy was so great they held a banquet in her honor on the following day. The feast was overfull with food and drink, including fruit, wild game, pies, pastries, and the finest sweet wines in the Kingdom. A host of lords and ladies sat in attendance, flanked by the bravest warriors in the land. All rejoiced, save one, whose brow was furrowed with sorrow.

18

CHAPTER 03

AVTANDIL'S CHALLENGE

The celebrations following Tinatin's coronation offered no seat for the sad or distraught. Yet, one of her guests sat with his head down. The mask he usually wore to hide his emotions had slipped, despite this man being surrounded by warriors and advisors he had spent a lifetime with. Now, the field of years across his forehead was plowed with fresh lines of sorrow.

Some of the people around him began to whisper. They wondered what saddened him, for it was only one day since he crowned his daughter as King Regent. Two guests were particularly worried about his troubles, but they had no answer.

They were Avtandil, who sat closest to Rostevan's heart, and Sograt, who understood the King's mind best. Together they discussed the state of their Lord and decided he must be gripped by unpleasant thoughts. They knew none of their actions caused him to be so pale, though Avtandil further voiced his concerns.

"What brought such sorrow to our King on this most joyous of days? Come, Sograt, and let us find why our host is so displeased with us. It shames me to celebrate while he sits alone and grieving. Perhaps we may entertain him with some pleasantry."

The aged advisor thought for a moment and rose from his seat. He filled their wine cups and called the youth to follow him. They made their way to the King, casting themselves down upon their knees and looking up at him with smiling faces. Ever wise, Sograt spoke teasingly, with eloquent and playful mischief in his words.

"My Lord, you are a tragedy to behold. The smile has run from your face like wine from a soldier's cup. We, too, share your sadness. Only yesterday, your own daughter gave away your rich and costly treasure. Why bring such grief upon yourself? Better you did not make her King and spared your heart this pain!"

No one from his court would dare insult Tinatin, and Rostevan jerked his head up in shock when he heard what was said. Yet he burst out laughing when he saw the grinning faces of Avtandil and Sograt before him.

"I marvel at your courage and audacity! Those who speak ill of my daughter are liars and fit for the gallows!"

All three of them laughed at the bold words, but the King was still haunted by the shadow of sorrow. After a sip of wine, he shared the thorn in his heart with his friends.

"I am not concerned with wealth, and what better hand than Tinatin's to rule when I am gone? No, nothing about my daughter troubles me. Rather, the years of my age drawing down around me disturb my mind."

"I devoted all the days of my youth to Arabia and her needs. Yet nowhere in our Kingdom is a man who learned the knightly arts from me. Though Tinatin is without equal, God gave me no son. This pains my heart, for life is fleeting. None can compare with me in archery or the game of ball. Only Avtandil bears some small resemblance to my skill, and this only thanks to the little I taught him."

The proud and young Knight bowed his head in modesty when King Rostevan spoke. Yet the slightest of smiles crossed his face before he composed himself. Though he looked down to hide the flash of his teeth, he had been seen.

"Why do you smile so? Are you shy with me? Pray, tell me what is laughable in my words?"

The youth was caught but quick on his feet.

"My Lord, if you grant me leave, I will tell you. But I will not disgrace myself if my thoughts offend you. I do not wish to court your displeasure and beg you not ruin me by inviting bold speech."

Rostevan laughed at the audacity the young Knight spoke with.

"Why would honesty displease me? You have been like my son from a distance, and I often take pride in your accomplishments. Do not be afraid of me. Whatever you would say, accept my sovereign oath and speak without fear of reprisal. By the life of my beloved Tinatin, you are among equals."

When his Lord spoke, Avtandil smiled, and it was like the sun glistening across a sea of pearls.

"By your leave, I must say you should be more modest when boasting of your skill, for I stand before you as an archer. Beneath me rests the world, and I say, let us have a wager."

"A moment ago, you said none are like you in archery. To deny this would be in vain. So, I ask, will you compete with me to learn which of us is the better?"

Rostevan clapped his hands at the bold spirit of his Knight.

"Thus is the folly of youth shown! Let's not delay this contest, for I cannot allow your challenge to go unsettled between us! Say the word, and we will seal our vows."

"Do not be shy of your words now, beloved son of Arabia, for you will not hide from this. I will test you on the field tomorrow at dawn, where your armies will bear witness. We shall see whose praises will be sung on the fields!"

Then they laughed with one another and clasped hands, agreeing on their bet. Whoever was victorious would have his skill praised throughout the Kingdom. The loser would go three days in public with his head uncovered. On hearing the terms between Avtandil and their King, the soldiers raised their cups, laughing and cheering.

With the challenge accepted and the time of their contest agreed, they and the other merrymakers celebrated late into the evening. Though their bet was made in faith between men, a victor was still undecided. Heaven would judge what happened the next day, but the plans of God are often quite different than those of men.

CHAPTER 04

A CONTEST OF KINGS

The day of their challenge dawned bright and sunny, without a cloud in the sky. Avtandil arrived early to meet Rostevan and his armies, wearing crimson armor and riding a white steed. He wore a veil of gold links over his eyes, and his cheeks shone like cut ruby. He was accompanied by his most trusted advisor, Shermadin, who had been his best friend since childhood. Like his Lord, he was also skilled in the art of war.

A cheer went up from the army when their General arrived. He raised his hand high in answer, saluting them and inviting the King to begin.

Rostevan rode up, shouting commands to those arrayed on the field.

"Let twelve servants tend to my needs and give me arrows. Avtandil will be supported by Shermadin alone, for he is the equal of my retinue."

"Those who attend me will faithfully count the shots and the hits between us. Then, when the contest is finished, they will give us an unerring report of the results!"

He turned then and addressed the huntsmen and soldiers.

"Ride to the end of the plains and drive all manner of beast and bird you find towards us. Ring the fields so nothing can get away. For everyone else gathered here, we invite you to bear witness to our contest. May the best man be victorious!"

When he finished speaking, his hunters rode away, disappearing into the distance. The troops broke rank and moved to encircle the plain so no creature might escape the hunt. Boisterous and full of joy, they cheered as their King and his challenger came forward. Soldiers placed bets on who would be the victor.

Avtandil and Shermadin joined Rostevan as he gave orders to his servants.

"Come to us! Bring our best bows and prepare yourselves. Do not be shy in keeping count! We will learn who prevails this day!"

No sooner had they readied themselves than countless animals broke forth from the far edge of the field. Herds of antelope, goats, stags, and wild asses charged towards them. The Lord and his vassal immediately set to pursuing game, and their bowstrings sang as untiring arms endlessly fired.

Hunters and hunted stirred up so much dust it cast a pall over the sun, yet they did not stop. The two challengers rode on, sending arrows speeding into the animals. Every shot found its mark, and no beast struck took another step. Each time one or the other exhausted his ammunition, servants brought more.

Their horses galloped back and forth across the plain, moving with the grace of dancers as they drove their quarry before them. The herd ran before Rostevan like waves before a storm. Avtandil bent and twisted as he fired one arrow after another, supple and graceful as a spruce tree. They dyed the fields crimson from the blood of their kills, slaying so many creatures it made God wroth.

Those who witnessed the prowess of the two champions stared in amazement. They spoke among themselves, comparing the contestants to legendary heroes from the old world. But their praise was lost to the hunters. The victor was yet to be decided, and they were focused on besting one another.

They rode down game for hours, leaving a wake of fallen creatures stretching out behind them. However, when they neared the far edge of the plains, they came to a broad stream. Its bed was laden with rocks, and a dense wood crowded the opposite side of its banks. The beasts they chased fled into the woods and beyond their reach, for neither horse nor rider was able to give chase there.

Seeing their game flee, Avtandil and the King ceased their pursuit. They laughed and called to one another, each proclaiming himself as champion. They joked and played like children as they waited to hear who won.

When the judges arrived, everyone crowded around, eager to learn the results. They counted who had slain what and how the shots fell. Meanwhile, the soldiers murmured and muttered of bets and hopeful wagers.

Rostevan raised his hands when the count finished, silencing the crowds and commanding his servants to provide the total.

"Come and tell us who is victorious. Be direct, as we do not desire flattery!"

The judges bowed before their King and the mighty Avtandil before speaking.

"Do not think we seek to deceive you. You commanded us to speak the truth, and this is what you will receive. Though you may slay us, it will not change the result in any way."

"As ordered, we counted every creature brought down between you both. You killed more than two hundred animals, yet the Knight struck twenty more than you. He did not miss one which he aimed his bow at, and the beasts he slew did not move another step."

"Though of those shot by you, we finished many ourselves, leaving the earth bloodied. While the two of you are beyond the might of us gathered here, but we cannot compare you to him. Avtandil is the victor and our champion!"

The King listened to the results with no more concern than if they recounted a backgammon or chess game. Then, when they finished speaking, a cheer went up from the crowd. Soldiers shouted, throwing their helmets into the air, and banging fists on their shields. Yet none cheered louder than Rostevan.

He rejoiced at Avtandil's victory. The young Knight was a foster-son to him, and he loved the youth as a rose loves the nightingale. The two embraced as a father to a cherished son, and sorrow fled from the King's heart like melted spring snow. All signs of grief vanished from his face.

Though weary from the hunt, they celebrated with the soldiers, resting under the trees to cool themselves. They broke bread together and made merry. Meanwhile, the twelve servants waited nearby, and the armies ringed them all, countless as chaff.

As they laughed and retold the events of their contest, Shermadin stepped away and let his eyes wander to the stream and forests beyond. His gaze followed the water as it wound off to the farthest edges of the glens. In the distance, he saw a strange Knight, seemingly lost to sorrow. Concerned at the appearance of a stranger, he called out to Avtandil.

CHAPTER 05

THE STRANGE KNIGHT

Shermadin called out to Avtandil and Rostevan, gesturing towards the young Knight weeping in the distance. The servants and soldiers turned as well, their eyes resting on the stranger. They admired him from afar, wondering where he had come from and marveling at his appearance.

The man was armored and wore a long coat with the skin of a spotted panther draped over his shoulders. In one hand, he held a whip thicker than a man's arm and the reins of a magnificent midnight black horse in his other. His steed's saddle and armor were covered in shimmering pearls. Yet for all his splendor, the burgundy rose of his brown cheeks was frozen by tears welling up from a woe-stricken heart.

Curious to know who this stranger was, the King sent one of his men to bring him. When the King's man approached, he realized the Knight was sitting with his head down. A shower of crystal rained from his eyes, and the servant was not able to think of any way to address him. After a time, he moved closer and spoke.

"My Lord commands your attendance. Come, and I will escort you to him."

Yet the dark-skinned stranger continued weeping, ignoring the servant's words, and acknowledging nothing. He did not even appear to hear the shouting from nearby soldiers. Intead, his mind drifted in a far land as his heart burned with unquench-able fire. The man was lost to the world and unaware of his surroundings. Tears welled forth from his eyes as though from floodgates. Despite the messenger repeating his request, he failed to pluck the bouquet of speech from the Knight's lips. Defeated, he returned with news of his failure.

"Lord, I delivered your message to the strange Knight, yet he does not respond. Though I was amazed by the sight of him, my heart was troubled by his pain. I stood beside him for a long time, but he did not realize what was before him. He weeps with-out end, and I was unable to learn why."

When Rostevan received this explanation, he became an-gry. This Knight in panther skins was no more than a wander trespassing on his lands. Who was he to dare refuse the Lord of Arabia? Then, turning to the twelve warriors who had attended him at the contest, he ordered them forward.

"Take up your weapons of war and bring me this one who dares ignore the summons of a King. I will have answers from him, whether he comes of his own will or by force."

The servants prepared themselves in a battle formation, coming towards the weeping Knight as one. As they neared, the clank of their armor had an effect where words had not. The youth raised his eyes to the warriors facing him. Where before he wept a stream, now rivers flowed from his eyes. He shouted out in pain before wiping the tears from his eyes.

"Woe is me!"

Then he readied his saber and quiver, mounting his steed and showing no intent to heed those around him or their cause. Their troubles, like these lands, were neither his nor his concern. He tried to ride past them and away, but they had other orders. The will of their King would not be denied.

They stretched out their hands to detain him, and in one movement, he fell on them like a wolf among lambs. He slew them all, beating one against the other. Some he struck with his whip, while others he cleaved down to the bone. His attacks were so ferocious even the enemies of those poor men would have pitied their deaths.

Rostevan was helpless to stop the slaughter, and his anger

turned to fury at the carnage unfolding before his eyes. Filled with wrath, he sent a legion of his best warriors to bring down the arrogant stranger. Yet, the Knight did not acknowledge the men chasing him, save the few who came too close. Those he threw down man upon man, each struck dead by the ferocity of his blows.

Though he far outmatched those trying to take him down, the army was slowly surrounding him. Soon he would be trapped, and he desperately sought an escape route, but the King and Avtandil understood his plans. They leaped to their mounts, closing off any hope of his exit. Although no one else had managed to overcome the youth, he would not be able to match the combined might of both Heroes at once.

The young stranger turned when they were near and realized he would soon be overtaken. In an instant, he raised his hand, striking his steed and disappearing. He vanished from sight, swallowed by the ground, or flown to Heaven. None could say where he went.

The King's warriors called the huntsmen, and they spent hours searching for any trace of the stranger. They rode far across the plains, but no one found a single sign of where he had gone. Some wondered if they chased the path of a man or a spirit.

While they continued looking, other soldiers cared for the injured. They bound the wounds of those few who survived the blows of the strange Knight and mourned the countless others who had been slain. Of all who lamented the loss of friends and comrades, none were more distraught than Rostevan. His men were surprised to see him crying over the dead without shame or concern.

"Everything is clear to me now. God has grown weary of the happiness my days have brought me. He who gives all has seen fit to sour my pleasure with the gall of bitterness. But, by his grace, whatever he desires will be. Now his hand wounds me to death, and I will seek no more joy from this world."

In all his years, the King had suffered no greater pain than what burdened him now. He was a man lost to sorrow. His heart was caged by the senseless deaths of his soldiers, leaving his spirit like a bird without wings. Crushed, he turned and rode away from his friends, advisors, and servants, returning to the castle. Full of mourning, he retired alone to his chambers.

Those who celebrated and played only hours before were now left groaning and crying. They could not decide what to do or where to find solace. Some agreed with their Lord and cried to God at why such a thing as this should be. Others hoped for an answer from their General, but Avtandil was not with them. He was worried for the safety of their King and had followed him back.

Once there, he came to the King's rooms and sat just inside the door, where he turned away all who came. Like the sound of music and celebration, the visitors soon stopped. With the silence, no semblance of merriment remained in the palace. It was then Tinatin received news of her father's sorrow.

CHAPTER 06

A DAUGHTER'S WISDOM

When Tinatin learned of her father's crippling sorrow, she came directly to his rooms. Outside of his door, she was greeted by his chamberlain, who stood and bowed before her. She asked the man about her father.

"How is my father? Does he sleep, or is he awake?"

"My lady, your father sits and broods like a man struck in the head. Even his color has suffered a change. Only Avtandil is with him, attending to his needs and turning away all who would disturb the King. I am told a strange Knight crossed their path and brought much ruin and woe. This appears to be the cause of the King's melancholy."

She nodded her understanding.

"If he is not injured, I will take my leave. Now is not the time for me to approach him. Yet, when my father asks where I am, you must tell him I was here a moment ago. When this happens, send for me, and I will come."

With these words, she returned to her apartments. Before long, Rostevan called the man and asked about his daughter.

"What news of Tinatin? Where is my solace and jewel, the water of my life?"

"She was here just now, my Lord, pale and full of worry but feared to interrupt your rest. So now she waits for you."

"I cannot bear her absence! Call her, and say, 'Sweet child, you are the life of your father. Why did you turn back? Come and drive away his grief. Heal his wounded heart. He will tell you why his joy has fled.'"

When she received his message, Tinatin came. She was worried but planned what she would say to console her father. When she entered his room, he set her by his side and kissed her forehead.

"Why did you stay away from me? Were you waiting for me to call you?"

"Father, you are King. Who, however bold, would dare approach you knowing of your sorrow? No doubt your suffering has dimmed the lights of Heaven, but I am sure we will find a solution together. But, I wonder, why did your men not solve this difficulty?"

On hearing her words, he showed the slightest of smiles.

"Sweet child, no matter my grief at this sad affair, the sight and life of you gives me cause for joy. You have lifted my spirits as though I've taken an elixir. However, when I tell you what happened, you will understand the reason for my sighing and groaning. Listen, and I will share my tragedy."

"When my contest with Avtandil finished, Shermadin pointed to a strange and beautiful youth at the far edge of the stream. This man was like a ray of light, brightening the Heavens and expanding the bounds of the earth. He wore the skin of a panther, and though he was a joy to see, some tragedy afflicted him. We did not understand what troubled him because he wept endlessly. So, I sent a messenger to bring him, but he refused my summons."

"His arrogance drew my wrath, and I ordered soldiers to seize him. When they approached, he wiped the tears from his eyes and mounted his horse to ride away. My men tried to stop him, but they were utterly destroyed by his hand. Seeing this, Avtandil and I rode to overtake him, but when we were close, he disappeared. Not once did he salute me as a man, and I cannot say if he was a man or Devi."

"We searched everywhere for this strange Knight but found no sign of him or his passing. When I counted how many dead were left in his wake, I realized my actions had turned the tender mercies of Heaven against me. Now, everything reminds me of those men on the field. I fear the days of my joy are brought to ruin. Though I may live long, I think nothing will give me cause to rejoice again."

When he finished speaking, Tinatin kneeled before him. She took his hands in hers, looking up at his sad face before offering him a solution.

"Why do you accuse God of bitterness towards you when he is tender to all? To what end would the creator visit this evil on you? Do not let your discontent with Fate leave you so upset. Cease your sadness. The boundaries of your empire span from one sea to the other, and you are King. Send your men to every village and town with news of your story. Soon you will learn the truth of whether he is a mortal man or something else."

"If this Knight in the panther skin is of flesh and blood, others will have seen him wandering the Kingdom. They will tell you where he is. Yet if no one has information, you can be certain he was a Devi. They are an old race and not like us. Their goals and desires are not something God has given us the ability to understand. Knowing this, you can forget the evil he sought to visit on you."

Rostevan thought long about what his daughter said. Her words were like the voice of chimes on the wind. They brought wisdom from Heaven on the wings of God's own angels. She stilled his mind and filled him with peace and serenity.

He smiled at her before calling his generals to him. When they arrived, he ordered soldiers sent to scour every part of the land.

"Go to the four corners of the world and search for this youth. Spare yourselves no pain, and do not delay in returning with the news. Allow no one to stand in your way and nothing to hinder you. Wherever you cannot pass, send a letter, and I will open the way. If a year passes and you do not find him, return here and tell me."

Over the following weeks, tens of thousands of men rode out from the palace in every direction. They went across Arabia and some into lands beyond. Months passed, and soon nearly all the time given to their search was gone, yet not a soul had found the man they sought. Bitter with their failure to find the Knight and weary of heart and mind, the men began trickling back to deliver their reports to the King. One after another, they told of their inability to locate the stranger until the last of them returned.

"My Lord, we have been unable to serve you, for there is no news. We wandered far in our search but found no living man or woman who has seen the Knight. We are sorry to give you no cause for celebration, but you must make another plan to catch this man you seek."

Yet, much to their surprise, the King was overjoyed.

"My daughter was right! The man was no more than a hideous and unclean Devi. I will not allow an evil spirit to deceive me into grief. Let us rejoice the passing of these dark days, for the burden around my neck is released!"

Though the soldiers and King's advisors were surprised at the sudden announcement, they were happy their Lord was back to his former self. Bright banners were hung across the city, and banquets of food and drink were prepared. Minstrels and acrobats performed in the streets, while sportsmen entertained the people with contests and feats of strength. Early in the afternoon, gifts were given freely to citizens and nobles alike.

Of all those celebrating, none were happier than Avtandil. Rostevan was like a father to him, and sons forever carry the burdens of their fathers. More, he felt responsible for the tragedy, as he was beside the King when the strange Knight vanished. But now, the weight of his failure was lifted, and he celebrated until the festivities began to wind down.

In the evening, he returned to his chambers. Watching as the moon rose, he readied himself for bed yet stopped short of going to sleep. He was still too full of joy and decided to play his harp. Wearing nothing more than his undergarments, he sat on the sofa, singing to himself as he played a quiet song. Then much to his surprise, someone knocked softly on his door.

Looking out, he was speechless at finding one of Tinatin's servants. The man whispered a message to him.

"The moon-faced one sends for you."

CHAPTER 07

AN UNEXPECTED GIFT

No more than a knock at the door, and the world fell from Avtandil's feet. Like a steed galloping across an open plain, his heart raced within his chest. He had never met Tinatin alone. There were always prying eyes in the Kingdom. No one was aware of his secret, but, despite the late hour, the ache in his soul would not let him resist her summons.

The pain of keeping silent about his love had grown greater with every new dawn and dusk separating him from her. Often, he felt himself more like a brother to the sun than a man. Each of them was shackled with chains, trapped, and eternally yearning for the moon, yet never able to reach her. An ocean might be measured from the tears he shed to quench the fires within, but he had never succeeded. Now, her invitation set him ablaze.

As he considered what to wear, he imagined putting a crown of fire on his head and giving her a bouquet of stars. Smiling to himself at his mortal limitations, he settled for dressing in his best clothes. He hoped his joy would shine as brightly as any Heavenly gifts he might have otherwise brought.

Despite the late hour, he left his room with bold steps. He answered to none but Tinatin and Rostevan, and only a fool would deny her. As he followed the servant towards her chambers, his spirits soared with thoughts of looking on the woman he loved.

When he entered, she quietly greeted him, and he carefully seated himself. Alone with her for the first time, he gazed into the depths of her eyes. To his surprise, he found a storm of mourning was brewing within them.

She sat next to the window like a wounded nightingale. A priceless red veil hid the rose of her lips, and she wore a gown of unlined ermine, but Avtandil did not count these baubles. His thoughts were entangled in the long tresses of hair twined around her pale throat, and the onyx of her eyes pierced his heart.

When his head cleared, he wondered at her sorrow before gathering the courage to ask.

"How can a man speak with one such as you? My mind departs, leaving me without leisure to think. I am utterly consumed and fear my tongue will betray me, yet I must learn what disturbs you. How may I help?"

Tinatin looked at him, choosing elegant and modest words before speaking.

"Although you have always remained far from me, I am surprised to see you meek or timid for a moment, but you are correct. There is something you can do for me."

"A malady afflicts me like a plague. It wounds my heart and leaves me in constant sorrow. I cannot stop thinking of the day you and my father killed game on the plain."

"I was told tales of a strange Knight in panther skins who refused to speak. Do you remember this youth who wiped the crystal of his tears away before disappearing? I have been as prey to thoughts of him. How is it one capable of standing against you and my father could be so distraught? He gave neither challenge nor contest to you. Instead, he fled the field. But why?"

"My father believes he was a Devi, as none of his soldiers found any sign of a man, but you and I know differently. If the goal of this stranger was to ruin our King, he would not have run from battle. So, I ask you, my Knight, to seek out this man and learn what ails him. Find out whether he really is a monster. Perhaps he may even be a brother in arms."

"Go beyond the borders of Arabia, and search for three years. Travel far and wide, through all the earth and bounds of the Heavens in service to me. Should you find him, return singing of your victory. Yet, if you who has no equal among my Knights are unable to do this, I too will believe he was no more than a Devi."

"I understand this task is great, but do not think I am so callous as to ask so much of you and give nothing. Until now, I never had the chance to sit in private with you, but I am not blind. I have seen more than you might be aware. You have been patient and virtuous, and your reward will be greater than what I ask. But first, I must share my own secret with you."

CHAPTER 08

TINATIN'S SECRET

"I know you are in love with me. There is no lie in saying this. Your heart is my captive, and you are my prisoner. Tears flow from your eyes without pause, and your soul is rent by my absence. I am certain you cannot escape this Fate because I am also slain thousands of times over. Perhaps you might ask yourself what King wants for lovers, but you would be misguided. I am no stranger to admiration from afar, but I have always belonged to you. Until now, I alone have kept this knowledge."

"Yet only you have the strength to complete the task I ask, so our love must remain in secret for now. I know this is a heavy burden, but only you can free me from this sadness. Slay the foul demons plaguing my mind and plant the violet of hope in my heart once more. Do this for me, and in doing so, strengthen the ties that bind us to one another."

"I swear to wed no husband other than you. Even if an angel comes from Heaven for my sake, I will perish first. In all the earth, there is no other man than you, my lion. Thus, strew roses on your path when you return, and I will meet you like a ray of sunlight. You will find your rosebud unfaded, for I am yours forever."

"Should I break this vow for any reason other than death, love would pierce my soul with a lance and bury my joy. I would be cut off from paradise and swallowed up by hell for eternity."

Tinatin's words burned away the chains weighing on Avtandil, and when he answered, his voice was thick with emotion.

"My skies were dark and moonless for so many years. Often, I thought death would be preferable to life without your heart, but today you have set me free. You have lifted the weight on my soul and given me new life. I might ask what I did to make you suspect me, but wiser men than I have known better than to question a woman's intuition."

"I will learn of this Knight in the panther skin, obeying you in this task as the planets obey the sun. Nothing will turn me from my quest, and I will be more faithful to you than any servant. Though the wall of the world may stand in my way, I will not wither, for your rays shine generously upon me. Should I grow weary of the long road, I will remember your eyes, which cause jet and onyx to blink. When I am done, I will return to you."

Having shared their hearts, they stared into each other's eyes and reaffirmed their oaths, holding hands for the first time. Avtandil would ride to the ends of the earth and search for the strange Knight, and Tinatin would wait three years for him. They made their covenant, promising a duty to one another no one would be able to come between.

Each had secretly grieved for the other all these long years, and now, their discovery of mutual love was like dawn breaking the dark of a night sky. Their smiles lit the room like flashes of lightning, and they talked for hours. They spoke of a hundred things, from nothing to everything, as lovers do.

Between words, the ruby glow of their faces revealed volumes shared between their eyes. When morning teased the edges of the horizon, they knew it was time to part. Though leaving was painful, their duty now was to honor and respect the vows they swore to one another. Before going, Avtandil turned to her once more.

"Though I must leave, it pains me to be away from you. I am a man driven to madness at the sight of your beauty and burned to ash by your fires. Be sure I will carry this task to completion and return to you." The young Knight turned then and walked away, but the pain of parting was more than he was able to endure. Though he had exchanged his heart for hers, it did not lessen the hurt of leaving. A hail of crystal tears rained down from his eyes, and sobs shook him like a palm at the edge of a storm.

Now more than ever, he longed to be beside her, but the door was closed. She was a King, and he a Knight. Each had matters to attend to, and neither owned the freedom to depart their responsibilities.

Resolutely placing one foot before the other, he forced himself home one step at a time. He lamented the hand fate had dealt him, sighing a private farewell until he might be with her again.

"The bite of her absence shows itself too soon on me. My soul is faded, and I have become more yellow than amber. I wonder, how will I survive all these years when I cannot gaze at her face? It will be like an eternal winter for me. Surely death is a better fate for lovers than separation, yet what other course do I have than that God has set before me?"

He continued speaking to himself until entering his chambers and falling into bed, still wearing his fine clothes. Unable to stop his tears, he sobbed, shaking like the leaves of an aspen tree on the wind, until sleep took him. In his dreams, he reached out to Tinatin, but she faded from his grasp, becoming no more than fog. Finally, when he could not hold her, he woke with a shout.

The reality of his oath weighed heavily on him, leaving his heart more tender than a new rosebud. For three years, he would be away from his love. This knowledge sat on his chest like a mountain. Nevertheless, though sorrow cloaked his soul, he began preparing for the long road ahead.

CHAPTER 09

A MEETING WITH THE KING

As General of the armies, he could not simply leave the Kingdom without permission from Rostevan, so he went to see him.
When he entered the audience hall, Avtandil learned the King
was busy. Frustrated, he gave a brief message to the chamberlain.

"I venture to tell you my thoughts these days and hope to
share these words in private."

With his request sent, he turned his mind to the lie he must
tell his foster father. If he did not misrepresent himself, he would
never be allowed to go. In all his life, he had not once lied to
those he loved, and doing so now pained him. But he had no
choice in the matter. Like all lovers, he was lost to matters of the
heart. Bereft of reason, his only course was to betray the trust of
those who mattered most to him.

In time he was escorted to his Lord. Once inside, he began
weaving the tapestry of falsehood he needed to support his lie.

"I have thought long on the might of our Kingdom. All
within the vast expanse of our borders bow to your rule. Yet,
many outside our walls are not subject to you. They do not know
of Tinatin's accession to the throne, which may create a problem
one day."

"With your blessing, I would like to carry these tidings
to all, including those beyond the far frontiers. To the obedient,

cause for celebration and rejoicing. Those who are disobedient will be made to weep before your power. I will wage war on them with my sword, piercing the hearts of your enemies and announcing her rule."

On hearing this from his beloved young Knight, the King praised him.

"Your counsel matches your valor, and your words are not so different than those of my wise advisor Sograt. Truly you are the Lion of Arabia! Hence, you may go and stretch your sword arm, though I wonder what I will do if you are gone long from these walls? You are like a son to me, and I am filled with joy when you are close."

Avtandil bowed deeply, hoping the red of his face was seen as humility and not shame at the half-truths he told.

"Your praise is an unexpected gift and warms my heart. With such blessings, perhaps God will lighten the darkness of our separation. I will send exotic gifts as I travel and hope it will not be long before I look once more on your radiant face."

With sweet words and deep affection, they embraced as father and son. The King kissed him farewell, and Avtandil made his way out of the throne room. To the youth, their ways were separated, and he was free to pursue his duty to Tinatin. Rostevan, wise and gentle, did not show the hurt his departure caused him. Instead, he turned away and hid his tears when the young warrior left.

Unaware of how he draped sorrow over Rostevan's heart, the Knight set off on his quest. His mind was of a singular purpose now. He would uphold his vow, and nothing would stand in his way.

CHAPTER 10

AVTANDIL'S CONFESSION

For twenty days, Avtandil rode across the Kingdom. He journeyed without pause, often riding through the night. In his heart, every step forward was one closer to Tinatin, the treasure and joy of his world. Nothing would steer him from his course or the fulfillment of his vows. He was neither cold nor tired, as the fires of love within kept him warm and filled with vigor.

Wherever he went, people welcomed his arrival with drums and celebration. Both commoners and nobles gave him generous gifts, adoring his presence and lamenting his passing. But joy though it was to be adored by those loyal to him, he wasted no time in reaching his destination.

Eventually, he came to the farthest edge of the Arabian frontier. He stood before an imposing fortress that struck terror in those who dared challenge the might of Arabia. The structure was built of solid rock, with towering stone walls stretching as far as the eye could follow.

This spot marked the end of the beginning of his journey. Once he passed the gates on the other side, he would be adrift and alone. The whims of Gods and Devils would be his to overcome, and he would be master and servant to no more or less than the skill of his own hand.

When he entered, Shermadin greeted him. This was the warrior he had been raised with, the same man who helped him with the contest against Rostevan, and he trusted him more than

than anyone else. They ate and drank together before inspecting the fortifications and greeting the soldiers. Then, when Avtandil had confirmed all was well, he invited his friend to speak in private and bared his soul.

"We have been inseparable as brothers these many years, and I come before you in shame. You alone are aware of my most secret affairs, yet you have not seen how I suffered and cried in silence. Until today, I could not to share this hidden woe with you, but now I tell you of my pain with joy."

"I have longed for Tinatin from afar. My heart was her prisoner, but now she has given me hope. Not long past, we shared our love of one another and swore an oath before I left the palace. I am sworn to spend three years beyond our borders to learn news of the strange youth in panther skins you and I saw so long ago. In return, she vowed to accept no man other than me and forever be my wife."

"To you above all, I must share what is in my soul, for only you understand me. My wish and duty are to my lady, but before anything else, I am a Knight. A vassal must serve, for faithfulness to Kings is fitting for those like you and me. We must not bend before misfortune but instead meet our fates as men."

"Of all the lords and vassals of Arabia, you and I are closer than brothers. So, I give you these words from my own mouth. While I am gone, I will appoint you as General over my armies. I can trust no other with this task. In my absence, you must lead the soldiers to battle and rule the nobles. Send messengers to court and state the affairs of the borderlands. Write letters as if you were me and present priceless gifts in my name, for why should anyone understand I am not here?"

"I ask you to keep this secret and await my return. Though I realize this is not a desirable task, mourn my passing and weep for me if I fail to come home. Sigh at the brother and friend you lost and inform the King of my death. Come before him as though you are drunk from sorrow and tell him the thing which none escape has befallen me. Give all my treasures of gold, silver, and copper to the poor, dispensing them among those who have not."

"More, I beg of you, should this tragedy come to pass, do not forget the childhood we shared. Be motherly in your heart towards me, and remember what was good between us, my dear Shermadin. Think often of the times we spent together and pray for my soul."

"In this, my brother, you will serve me best."

CHAPTER 11

THE LAMENT OF SHERMADIN

Shermadin cried out in denial when he heard what was planned, begging his friend to consider a different course of action.

"Why must you face the dangers of our frontier without aid? I will accompany you, and we will ride away from the Kingdom together. Do you not think I would prefer the earth to cradle me beside instead of knowing you were alone when you needed my help most?"

Seeing Shermadin's anguish, Avtandil tried to calm him. Yet he could not, and they argued back and forth. One intent on accompanying the brother he loved, and the other set to leave in the morning. Eventually he spoke again.

"Listen to me, for I speak a truth free of any falsehood. When a lover would roam the fields, he must wander by himself. Pearls do not fall to those unwilling to buy and bargain for them. You know this as well as I do, for these truths are part of the lance which pierces the evil and treacherous. It is the way of Knights."

"Fine. Clearly, your mind is set, so it is beyond me to stop you, but no one will believe this lie. How can I imitate you or resemble you as lord, and who among our men will not see through the deception? Why do you need to appoint me in your stead anyway?"

"You know there is no other I can share my secret with. More, who could act as well as you in my absence? You are the only one I trust to fortify the borders and keep our enemies from breaching the walls. The whole of our Kingdom is in your hands. If God does not make me wholly lost, I will return, but what I ask of you is a duty between us. As for how people should believe you, this is simple. I will give you a letter. Whoever is my courtier must obey your word as mine, but you must not forsake me in this."

"And if I do this, what of us? How will I find any measure of peace when I know my brother faces the world alone? Who will help you if you fall or become ill?"

"We are both aware that hazard kills all men equally. It does not matter if it is one or a hundred things. If Heaven protects me, nothing will deter me, and if not, it is in God's hands. I am sorry, but this is the way it must be."

Though he was not pleased with the idea, Shermadin saw the truth of Avtandil's words. He could think of no other solution, and his friend would not be swayed. So, they agreed one would defend the Kingdom and the other search for the Knight in the panther skin.

They clasped hands and made their vows to one another. Afterwards, they spent the evening together, remembering the years of their adventures and life. The words between them were like spring flowers on a cherry tree. Each was as different and unique as a sun setting into the sea, yet all brought to the same end. Avtandil would not change his mind, and all blossoms eventually fall.

Shermadin took joy in their shared memories, though it was tinged with the bittersweet sorrow of soon parting. He would carry this burden. For it was the duty of Knights and brothers to aid one another.

CHAPTER 12

EARTH BENEATH YOUR FEET

The next day dawned bright and sunny, without a cloud in the sky. Avtandil prepared himself and readied gear for his journey. Then he called Shermadin and gave him a letter tied with gold and sealed with wax. This would be read to the armies when they realized their general was gone. Until then, it would be kept away.

When the Knight came out, he looked across the men formed into lines outside the gates. Their presence moved him, and he saluted them before speaking.

"Your duty and service warm my heart. Today I will inspect the fields alone and return when I am finished. I need none as a companion, and Shermadin will remain in command until I am back."

His men dispersed, and after the last of them left, he clasped hands with his friend and rode away from the wall and into the frontier. For three days and nights, he went on, his horse galloping over the plains like a wave racing towards a distant shore. Soon he would be farther from Arabia than he had ever gone, but his thoughts did not rest on the road ahead. He could not stop thinking of Tinatin, who kept his heart. She was what he desired most, despite every step forward taking him away from her.

On the evening of the third day, his soldiers began searching for him. Those with swift horses scoured the area surrounding the fortress, while others took to the walls. But though they ran and shouted for the lion who was their Lord, none found any trace of his passing.

When Shermadin learned of this, he assembled the courtiers, nobles, and soldiers. Then, he brought out the letter and read it to them. The words were as follows:

"My vassals, instructors, and those among you who are my pupils, you are all faithful, trusty, and tried. Each of you has been attentive to me like shadows, and now I ask you to listen. For I, Avtandil, the earth beneath your feet, write this with my own hand."

"A matter requires me to depart alone and journey to a far country. I will travel for some years, trusting my bread and meat to bow and hand. I ask only to return and find the realm unshaken by our foe."

"In my stead, Shermadin is appointed as your lord. You know how he has grown with me, as a brother and as a son. Thus, I command you, obey him as though he were me. Let him sound the trumpet and do all as I have done before. Until he learns of my life or death, may he shine upon you like the sun."

Though the words of their Lord left the men heart-pierced, they did not question his appointment of their new leader. Instead, each man paid homage and swore obedience. Although everyone would miss Avtandil, none wished him home safely more than Shermadin. Sadly, their wishes could no more become horses than beggars could ride them. Now, only the passing of time would tell which path Fate chose.

CHAPTER 13

THE ROAD BEHIND

Avtandil left the plains of the Arabian frontier, flying at an impossible pace in his haste to find news of the mysterious Knight in the Panther Skin. He roamed over foreign lands and into places unseen by him or anyone he knew.

His road was long, and he often reflected on the predicament he was in. Separation from Tinatin robbed a part of his life, but he pressed on, crossing from one country to the next as the days stretched into months.

Though he was friendly to everyone he met, none of them knew about the man he sought. Between towns and cities, he asked news from merchants, travelers, and wayfarers, but learned nothing from them. No matter where he looked for information, he found nothing.

As the seasons marched into the second winter, his heart became tattered and forlorn. Loneliness took its toll on him, and fresh snow blasted his frozen soul. At times he cried out in agony from the pain and solitude of his plight, lifting his knife to the sky and shouting.

"Dionysius and Eros, you who witnessed the rose of my love blossoming, can you not see me? Where is your aid to lovers who have become lost? I am far from her, who the fabled ruby of Badakhshan cannot compare, and all joy has fled my heart. These bones ache for home and hearth, yet I have no harp nor lyre or pipe to soothe me."

But his cries were never answered. His sorrow went unnoticed, and he was left with no choice other than to continue his journey. To him, it felt he carried the weight of the world, balanced as it is between the vows of lovers.

In time he crossed strange lands and distant places. The earth became a couch to him, and his arm a pillow. Sometimes he could only go on by reminding himself to be patient and trust in God. Meanwhile the reed stem of his form faded into ruin with the endless procession of days.

The burden of his quest rent his spirit like a rose separated from the sun. He missed Tinatin more with each passing day and often spoke aloud, with none but his horse to hear his words.

"I am far from my beloved. Though my heart stays with her, perhaps my death would be a mercy. It would spare her from sharing the torment and pain of our separation."

He rode all over the face of the world, leaving no place beneath Heaven where he had not been. Yet, no one had knowledge of the Knight he sought. The days flew by, a constant reminder of the leagues he crossed.

Seasons came and went like the wind. Spring bled into summer and died with the kiss of autumn. As the golden leaves fell and were forgotten, the land became lost once more to the barren wastes of winter. Still, the road to nowhere continued to stretch before him. Eventually flowers blossomed again, and he counted his journey as spanning nearly three years with no sign of an end.

In time he crossed into a rough and dreadful land. For a month, he did not meet a single son of Adam or daughter of Eve. All he found were wild beasts until he began to become more beast than man. More alone than at any time before, he considered the weight of his woes and believed they even surpassed those of Vis and Ramin. All he could think of was his beloved and the day he would return to her arms.

At last, he came to a towering mountain and found a resting place high up in the peaks. Looking down one side, he could see a nearly endless plain stretching to the horizon. On the other, a forest ran down to the edge of a deep and wide river he couldn't hope to swim.

As he made camp, he considered what lay ahead of him and what was behind. Of his three years, only two months were left, and he knew nothing of the Knight. If he met him, the journey would end, but how was he going to make someone appear who did not exist? It would be easier to turn evil into good or be born again by his own hand.

He sighed bitterly, calling out to God in frustration.

"Why have you taken the joys of life and love from me and left a nest of grief in their place? If I go home now, what was the purpose of my journey? Why have I wasted so much time? I have not learned a word of gossip concerning this Knight in the Panther Skin. How can I present myself without a whisper of what I vowed to seek?"

"If I stay here, I must continue searching, but what of my agreements? What if I travel everywhere and still find nothing? Shermadin will give news of my death to King Rostevan and Tinatin. The loss of me will be bitter to those I love. Meanwhile, I will make my friend a liar and lose the woman I sacrificed everything for. How can I return to the ashes of all I loved?"

Distraught and bereaved of heart, Avtandil finally slept. He was weary of roads and heartsick from longing for his beloved. Yet, in the morning, he woke from a dreamless sleep, rested and clear of mind for the first time in many months.

As he rubbed the sand from his eyes, his thoughts turned to how far he had come. He had much left to do and did not want to fail. Strengthening his fortitude, he drew a measure of peace from his surroundings.

"A man may conquer all the world, but in the end, time conquers all men. Without God, I can do nothing, for none can change what He has decreed. Those things which are not to be will not be. Therefore, I will not cast down my heart a day too soon. Better I find patience, or these many years will have flown away to nothing."

Lost in his thoughts, he broke camp and packed his belongings. Finally, his mood lightened. He sighed to himself, voicing a mix of hope and cynicism.

"Perhaps I should die, for it is preferable to living a life of shame. But, if I go back, Tinatin, who brightens the sunniest of days, will meet me. She will ask for tidings of that radiant youth. What will I accomplish if I have only my failure to complain of?"

"At the same time, why should I pity myself in vain if it offers no reprieve to my plight? I have passed every man and creature under the sun but learned nothing of this Knight. If he is a Devi or Kadj Sorcerer, perhaps I should be wondering what will become of me if we meet."

CHAPTER 14

DUTY IS A MOUNTAIN

Though Avtandil had come up the mountain easily, going down the other side proved considerably more difficult. The ceaseless babble of streams and murmur of trees on the wind frustrated, as did the many obstacles he was forced to overcome. Carefully choosing his path, he crossed through woods and over small ravines and rivers as he made his way down. By the time he reached the bottom, his pride and the power of his arms had been spent on the tricky descent.

He wanted to ride far from where he had been and picked out the route he would take, riding until he came to the top of a small hill. Looking out, he was amazed at the beauty before him. Though the lands he previously crossed were wild, God's hand clearly moved through this place. Jetties of stone stuck out from the undergrowth, and a field of brilliant red tulips stretched over plain like a sea of ruby. He could not think of a more beautiful place to end the tragedy of his journey.

This was to be his last road, for his duty was a mountain from which he could not escape. He would cross these fields, and then return to the Kingdom of Arabia. Tinatin and Shermadin held his honor, and he was beholden to them, having sacrificed too much to betray those he loved.

Though he yearned to put his steed to a gallop across the plains, hunger clawed at his belly. Deciding he needed to eat, he strung his bow and gave himself over to the task of hunting. When he brought down game, he made camp near the edge of the river. There, he used tiny twigs and dry grass for kindling a fire from the steel at his belt.

He rested himself on a soft bed of reeds while the meat roasted. His horse grazed, and he allowed his mind to wander the many roads he traveled to get here. He wondered aloud at Fate but expected no answer.

"How can a man find himself so far from home and still to no end. If God helps those who help themselves, why have I found no sign of the Knight I hunt? Perhaps he really is a ghost."

But his thoughts were soon interrupted by a band of six horsemen approaching from the west. He stood and readied his weapons before moving towards them. He considered why they were here, concerned as to who they might be.

"Who else besides bandits or thieves would I find in these far lands? No other men would seek such a place unless there was evil in their hearts."

Walking closer, he made out two bearded men carrying a younger and beardless man between them. Three others rode behind them like vassals, leading the horses of the men on foot. The young man's head was grievously wounded, but it no longer bled. Clearly, his soul rested on death's doorstep and his spirit had nearly faded. The two men holding him wept and grieved aloud.

Avtandil, keeping his distance in case they meant to ambush him, called out.

"Brothers, I mistook you as brigands. Who are you to come here, and what brings you to this distant land?"

They kept coming towards him, shouting as they came.

"We bear you no harm! Be calm and help our brother if you can. If not, pray and add your grief to ours. Complete our sorrow and weep with us who need pity. Scratch and rend your cheeks at the tragedy we carry between us."

Still wary, he approached them, helping to lay the wounded man in the soft grass. He spoke kindly to the strangers and asked of their plight. In turn, they explained what had struck the youth, sparing no detail as they recounted events.

"Our tears are because we three are brothers and lords of a populous and fortified town in the land of Cathay, Khataet'ti. We had been told of countless animals near this place and spent several days journeying here with a company of soldiers and wagons. We camped on the bank of a stream the first night, and then began our hunt. The rumors of game were true, and the hunting pleased us."

"For a month, we hunted, killing on the plains and in the mountains and ridges. We shamed our archers, for none of them could equal our skill. But we could not find the truth of who was the best among the three of us. Eventually we decided on a friendly challenge, and as is the way of siblings, ours was a contest of love. For who should win and yet still not be a brother?"

"Just this morning, we sent most of our men home, loaded with stags and hides. Save these three armor-bearers, all others from our retinue departed. We thought it safe to hunt among ourselves, as we had seen no other human."

"We rode everywhere, each hunting game in the sight of the other, free of onlookers. We went through woods and over streams, killing many wild beasts. Not a bird flew up which we did not bring down."

"Sadly, our mirth was short lived, for arrogance soon bade its hand towards us. Not knowing our folly, we invited ruin on ourselves. I cannot understand or explain the Devi who visited us. Yet you can see the plight of our brother before you and the sorrow we now carry."

With these words, the brothers wept while Avtandil bandaged the wounded youth. When he finished, they calmed themselves and told him of their tragedy.

CHAPTER 15

MY BROTHER BEFORE ME

"In the middle of our hunt, and seemingly from nowhere, a Black Knight appeared. The man was dark and morose, with a grim visage. It seemed as if smoke and mist had brought the spirits of the plains to life. He was seated on the blackest of steeds, which was armored and bedecked in jewels, somehow seeming to float."

"Clad in the skin of a panther, it as though he stepped from a vision. Surely no one ever witnessed such beauty in a man before, yet there he stood. Though his eyes were not kind towards us, a radiance emanated from him which we were unable to account for."

"He gazed on us, whip at his side, and without weapons in his hands. We were barely able to support ourselves under his gaze, for he was like a sun on earth, come down from Heaven. I cannot say why, but it came into our minds to seize him. Yet, venturesome as we were, the folly of our actions did not appear to us at once. This is the cause of our weeping, for we brought this tragedy on our own heads."

"Being the oldest, I begged my brothers to give me this man to fight. Next, my middle brother, who praised the skill of his horsemanship, made his claim. Yet, in the end, the youngest of us won. He sought only to conquer the man, and we fools gave this challenge to him. Now he rests before us at the gates of death's kingdom, but we did not understand then as we do now."

"As we approached the stranger, intent on taking him, he came towards us without changing his demeanor nor posture. Instead, he rode calmly, radiant as a star. His cheeks were ruby, mingled with the crystal of tears for reasons we do not know. Though his thoughts may have been indifferent or tender before we sought to take him, they quickly turned to wrath."

"He spoke no words in explanation and gave us no opportunity to escape. When our youngest attempted to engage him, the stranger grabbed him, but as he held no weapon, we kept back. How could we have realized his power?"

"He struck our brother with his whip, cleaving his skull in a single blow. A river of blood poured from his head, and he crumpled to the ground, collapsing like a stone as he met the earth. Then, having humbled him for his arrogance, the Knight turned and with bold steps slowly left. He did not look back, never speaking or raising a hand against us who remained standing. Perhaps he spared us the bite of his sword out of consideration, but it did not matter to our brother. His Fate was sealed."

The joyless men continued talking as they pointed to the horizon.

"Do you see him? He who is like the sun goes as he came, without haste. There is no care or concern for what is left in his wake."

At this, Avtandil looked up from the weeping brothers and their tragic tale. In the distance he saw a black silhouette of a man riding a steed of shadow into the approaching twilight. It was the man he sought for so long.

His earlier indecision faded to dust at the sight of his quarry. His quest had not been in vain, and his cheeks would no longer be covered in the snow of frozen tears as he fruitlessly scoured wastelands and barren plains. The myth he chased was before him, and with this, he found a new revelation. When a man attains what he wished for, past woes must be forgotten.

Perhaps it really was a Devi, but now he would find out. With these thoughts fresh on his mind, he turned and addressed the woeful brothers.

"For nearly three years, I searched for this Knight. In this time, I have been a wanderer without a place. I traveled far from home and all I love, but today I learned from you what I have been seeking. It is no easy thing you discovered for me. Truly I hope God never again gives you cause to grieve."

"I ride now to meet the wish of my heart's desire, but I would not see further suffering befall you or your brother. Go to my camp and eat the food I prepared. Give him and yourselves rest and take whatever you need. I will not return there, for must learn what darkness lies on this man's heart, or if he is even a man."

Mounting as he finished speaking, Avtandil spurred his horse forward. He flew across the plain like the moon racing to catch the sun, as though the wings of a hawk carried him. Seeing the stranger gave him new resolve. The fires which earlier burnt the reed of his form to ash were now extinguished.

CHAPTER 16

AS THE MOON CHASES THE SUN

Avtandil charged across the plains, closing the distance between himself and the Knight. As he rode, he wondered how best to approach the stranger.

"The man I chase has allowed no one to speak or reason with him. If he is a man, and not a Devi, perhaps he is mad. If I come to him now, it will only be for us to slaughter one another, for senseless conversation only enrages a madman more. In the end, either he will be more hidden to me, or I will be dead."

"Yet, I have not suffered these years in vain to learn nothing. All things must rest, so I will follow him until he stops. Then I will watch his behavior from a distance. If I am patient, I may determine what he is and find a way to meet him."

For two days and nights, they traveled in this manner. One riding before, and the other behind, like the moon chasing the sun. They were pitiable, despite their beauty and grace. One cried for his own mysterious reasons, and the other for both of their plights. Though weary, neither stopped nor rested.

On the evening of the third day, they came to a large forest surrounding a tall outcropping of rocks. A stream flowed from the peaks and wound off into the distance. This was where the dark stranger went. He passed through a wall of reeds and then beneath towering trees before making his way to the caves nestled in the heights.

Curious to see more before showing himself, Avtandil stopped at the edge of the forest and climbed a tree. From there, he watched as the Knight rode up and dismounted. On his arrival, a maiden wearing black came out to greet him. He embraced her neck with his arm before stepping away and crying out in woe.

"Sister Asmath, I fear all our bridges have fallen into the sea. We will never find her. She will be consumed and forever lost to us."

Tears rained from his jet lashes as he beat his chest in dismay, and the young woman fainted, but he caught her as she fell. When she woke, they cried together, their lament echoing pitifully from the rocks and hills.

Avtandil looked in wonder at their behavior. He had no idea what tragedy wounded them so profoundly, but now he was certain it was a man he chased. Though he heard the maiden's name, he still did not know who the man was. More, he did not know how he would learn more from either of them when they were both so distraught.

As he looked on, the maid composed herself. She removed the saddle and gear from his steed and led it into the cave. When she came back, she unbuckled the Knight's armor, which he carried in. She followed behind, and they did not come out again that day.

At dawn, still clothed in black, she brought the horse out again and saddled it, polishing the bridle with her veil before going back in. After a time, the Knight came out, and without a word, she helped him buckle his breastplate on. Neither of them made a sound, as though they prepared themselves for a funeral procession. When the buckles were done, she embraced him, and he kissed her forehead.

Then he turned and rode off, crossing the stream as he passed under the trees the same way he entered the day before. She cried as he left, her delicate shoulders crumpled beneath the weight of her grief.

The sight of him passing by moved Avtandil. Though the stranger's mustaches had hardly grown, he was a marvel to behold, shining like the son of Heaven. There were few men with such grace and strongly. Surely, he could kill a lion like a cat killing a mouse.

As the youth disappeared into the distance, an idea came to Avtandil.

"It would seem this Knight is often gone and never stays long, yet she spends her days in these caves. No doubt she is a prisoner to the sorrow her heart carries. Once he is out of sight, I will ride up, pretending to be him. Then, when she comes out, I will grab her and share my story."

"When she knows the truth of who I am, I can convince her to tell me his tale. In this way, I will not be forced to strike him with my sword nor be pierced by his. Truly, God could not have done better for me than this."

His course of action decided, he climbed down the tree and mounted his horse, riding to the mouth of the cave and making as much noise as possible. Almost immediately, the tear-faced girl ran out. She thought the sound of his steed was the return of the morose youth, but she was mistaken. She did not recognize the face of the man in front of her. He was a stranger and seeing him filled her with terror.

CHAPTER 17

BREAKING THE GIRL

She cried out at the sight of Avtandil, trying to flee into the trees, but she was not fast enough. He leaped from his horse and seized her like a bird in a net, wrestling her to the ground. She wailed at the loss of her freedom, as all wild things do.

Her cries echoed and resounded from the rocks as she thrashed back and forth and shouted for help. She hoped to escape, but she was trapped. Like a rabbit caught in the talons of an eagle, she could not break the cage of his arms. Though she yelled and cried, no aid came.

Yet, he had underestimated her will to fight. Too late, he realized the capture he planned would only end in breaking the girl. Because of this, he released his grip and instead held her hands tightly. She stood and he begged her to stop struggling. When at last she relaxed, her tears flowed like spring rains.

Understanding he had overstepped himself, he tried to calm her by explaining his intent.

"Do not cry. I did not come here to hurt anyone. Ask yourself, what harm can I do to you which I had not already intended? You are a daughter of Eve, and I am Avtandil, a son of Adam. All I want is the answer to a question."

"Today, you were with a man who has the face of an angel and the form of a spruce tree. You must tell me his story and who he is. This is all I ask, and I will leave you in peace."

She looked at him, thinking what a fool he was. He did not realize her depth of will or resolve, but he would soon learn. Slowly she stopped crying and gathered the strength to answer.

"You, who I do not know, present yourself as a Knight, yet it was your rough hands which caught and hold me still. Why would I trust you? What else will you do or request when you get what you want? If you are not a madman, let go of me, and if you are mad, return to reason before your doom comes."

"You ask me to tell you a private and difficult matter as if it were gossip, but this thing has never been written. Your time is wasted prying after what you cannot grasp. I will not be the vessel from which this story spills. Thus, stay your tongue, spare your hand, and release me."

Unwilling to accept no for an answer, he thought he could make her understand if he spoke from his heart. Bearing a piece of his soul, he asked again.

"You have no idea where I am from or the woes I endured to get here. For three years, I searched for this man you call brother. In all this time, I did not find anyone who saw him. Now I found you, and though I overstepped myself, I must learn his story. Do not be shy. Speak to me, for I will not let you go until you tell me."

Her voice turned towards the edges of anger as she spoke again. The words she responded with were sharp as daggers on the tender heart of Avtandil.

"You do not hear pleasant speech, so I will tell you directly. The sun you seek is not near us, but you knew this, or you would not dare to come here. There is nothing you can do to make me speak of him, no matter your actions! Now stop asking. Your questions annoy me like frost on the beard of an old man."

Desperate to learn about the strange youth, he threw himself down and begged. He repeatedly implored her to understand the sacrifices he made in search of the man she now protected. Yet, she refused him, each time more shortly than the last. Finally, he could bear no more.

His indignation peaked, flushing his face, and turning his eyes to madness. He rose from his knees, grabbing her by the hair and drawing his sword in a single motion. She yelled out, at first in pain and after with surprise as he held the blade against her throat.

"How can I forgive your ill will? I begged for nothing more than words. Where is the harm in telling me this story? I would continue begging at your feet, but I see now my tears would be in vain. Tell me what I have asked, now, and I will go. Yet, should you refuse me, I will cut the head from your shoulders and leave your corpse to rot here!"

Though she was at his mercy, her anger could be contained no longer. She was disgusted by the barbarism he displayed. Her body shook with fury, and her eyes lit with fire as she spoke.

"You far exceed yourself in threatening force against me. If you do not kill me, I will not die. Instead, I will wait until he who you ask of has returned. At that time, my woe will pass, and yours begin. Yet, if you put your sword to use, I will have no head with which to speak. You are a fool of a man, for whatever you do, you will not find the answers you seek."

"You deceive yourself into believing death would be the cause of my suffering. You understand nothing of me, and I do not know you. Better you bring ruin to me and end my misery, for it would release me from this endless weeping. The fjord of these tears might finally dry, and my wellspring of sorrow cease to exist. For there is no way you will compel me to give what is not mine to part with."

As the last words escaped her lips, she pressed her neck against his sword, bringing him to his senses. He was forced to step back and drop the blade, noticing a red line across her throat where he had abused her. Aghast at allowing his emotions overcome reason, he wrestled with what he had done to Asmath, wondering to himself how he would ever win her trust now.

"Truly, it is a poor man who bears the title of Knight and behaves as I have. In my haste and anger, I wronged a woman I meant no harm to. Now, how will I find a way to her heart so she will speak to me again?"

Defeated by his own mistakes and her sharp words, he released her. Burdened by shame, he walked away and sat down. Unsure of how he might warm her to his cause, he began to weep. The stress of his long years finally caught up with him, and he looked up. His cheeks were wet and forlorn, and he spoke to her without demands for the first time.

"I am sorry. You are right. I overstepped myself, and do not know the road home now. My actions offended and angered you, though my intent was far different. For this, I do not know how I will survive."

CHAPTER 18

A KNIGHT REVEALED

Asmath wept as she looked at the young stranger and wondered what to do about this man. He had held her against her will and threatened her life, yet he did not truly harm her. Of course, he did not give her any reason to forgive him, but her Knight was not so different than the man who sat before her. As her tears fell, she watched, and her heart began to soften.

She did not know his tale, though she knew well the story he asked her to tell him. Knowing one and not the other, she found pity for both. In truth, she too was part of the tapestry and suspected all of them shared sorrows woven of a similar tragedy. Rather than speak to him, she chose to wait, weeping in silence. For she knew, wisdom and patience were the hands of forbearance upon the brows of those wronged. It needed to be he who bridged the distance between them.

In time, Avtandil stood. He put down his weapons and walked towards her with no pride in his steps. Unlike a thief who bore sorrow only for the consequences of his actions, he came with humility and genuine regret. He was a man shamed by the knowledge and understanding of what he had done and why it was wrong.

He got down on his knees and bowed before her, the desperation and fire of his earlier demeanor gone. Meek as a willow bent before the storm of his wrongs, he apologized. For the first time, he spoke to her with the tongue of a Knight instead of a madman.

"I abused you in deed and word. By my own hand, I made you a stranger to me. Your anger is not misplaced, for my actions caused the loneliness I now suffer. Yet, the wise have said sin must be forgiven seven times. Knowing this, I hope to receive the grace of your forgiveness."

"Though I alone bear the blame for the wrong of my service, I beg you, pity the soul rent by love. Understand this. There is no other than you in all the world from whom I might find aid or draw strength. For the sake of my heart, I yield my life to you. What more can I do than this?"

When he mentioned love, Asmath began to sob uncontrollably. Her tears, which before had been soft as summer rain, fell like a waterfall. It seemed to Avtandil his wish had been granted. She was moved by his words, though it pained him to witness the ruin she suffered for it.

When her color changed, he understood she did not cry because of what he said. Instead, he thought she was wounded for one she loved. Indeed, he reasoned, she carried a madness about her not unlike his own. Seeing a chance to connect with her, he told his story.

"We share a bitterness and hurt which only love can cause. Yet you must know even foes have pity for the agony lovers endure. It compels them to seek death, ending the light of all joy and the fire of every pain. They do not turn away from the eternity of darkness, for it sets them free."

"I did not choose the path of daggers I walk. Love gave it to me and made me a madman. The sun of my life, Tinatin, sent me to find this Knight you call brother. I have not heard a cloud or whisper from her for near three years as I journeyed in search of him. This separation makes my life unbearable, yet to this day I have not forgotten or forsaken my vows to her."

"The face of your Knight is imprinted on my mind like a holy icon. I gave up all the joy of my life and became mad for him. Now I fear there are but two choices before us. Set me free or slay me. There is no other way open to me. Speak, and release me to one fate or the other, for I am your slave and can ask no more than this."

She looked up when he spoke, wiping the tears from her

raven lashes. Fixing her eyes on him, she gave him an answer more pleasant than he had any right to hope for.

"The words you share now are what I expect of a Knight. They are far better than the poison which you sowed enmity in my heart with earlier. The truth you speak begs me to forgive you, and so I do. More, your duty to another has won a friend and sister in me."

"As you called on love as your aid in this matter, I will devote myself to you. To behave otherwise would bring further sorrow and ruin to us both. Should I be unable to assist you, I would rather perish. For it is becoming of one held prisoner to the whims of love to help another who shares similar bonds."

"Now, quiet your heart and listen closely to what I say. If you follow my instruction, you will learn what you seek, and your quest will not fail. You will return to your Tinatin and be whole once more."

"Yet, if you refuse me and do not heed my words, the way before you will be forever lost. You will not find what you have so long sought. Instead, your tears will flow like rivers, and all the world will come down around your head. In the end, you will die in shame knowing it was your hand which brought everything you loved to ruin."

Her words moved Avtandil to the point he could not speak for a moment. He looked at her, remembering she called herself sister to him, and gave a small smile before answering.

"What you ask of me, I will do, and of what you said to me, I am reminded of an old tale of two men. They journeyed together somewhere along some road, and the one behind witnessed the one before fall into a deep well. He rushed forward, crying out, and told the man to stay so he might bring ropes to pull him up. From down in the well, his friend laughed and shouted back up, 'If I do not wait, where will I go? I am trapped. None other than you can save me. Without your aid, I am lost.'"

"I am like this man in the well and can do nothing alone. You are a balm to the madness which earlier consumed me. I would not willingly bind myself with ropes. Instead, I will follow whatever road you choose. As you are my sister now, so will I forever be your brother."

Asmath, pleased at his words, leaned close and took his hands. She stared into his eyes before answering.

"Your speech is more pleasant now than before. It would appear you are truly a good Knight, come from afar. Doubtless, you are worthy of praise in your lands and elsewhere. Since such grief has fallen on you once, I would not want to see it on your head again. Now, listen carefully, and you will find the answer to what you seek."

CHAPTER 19

THE THREADS BETWEEN US

"In all the world, there is no other place you will learn the story of this Knight. Yet, if he will not tell you what you seek, it will not be told. He carries the weight of this stone around his neck, and no other can give you the truth. If your words are sincere, wait here until he returns, and above all, be calm around him."

"No doubt you are eager to hear his name, so I will tell you. He is Tariel, rent and distracted by the tragedy he suffers. Me, you already met, though his pain struck my heart not once, but twice. The hottest of fires burn me. I am sure you have seen me sighing, for I am alone more times than you can count."

"Unfortunately, I cannot tell you much more of him. He roams the plains in search of what only he has the right to tell you. What I eat is brought by his hand. I am well cared for, but my days are spent in solitude. Though he comes and goes as he pleases, I can tell you he must come. Like you, he bears a duty from which no true man can escape."

"This is why you must wait. If you leave, who can say what you will find on your return? He might decide you were a brigand and bear arms against you. My soul would be rent over this, for the loss of him or you would pain me beyond words. By staying here, however many days it takes, you will give me time to plead with him."

"Perhaps I will be able to warm him towards you. In this way, you will meet one another without coming to blows. He may understand and love you, sharing his story. Then you can return to your Tinatin and give her cause to rejoice."

Though exhausted, he sat like a student to her words, submitting himself to what she knew, and he not. The two of them spoke until evening, discussing many things, until the sound of a rider disturbed them. Together, they looked out and saw Tariel approaching, carrying a freshly killed stag across the back of his horse.

He was magnificent on his black steed, tall and fierce, with a panther skin draped over his shoulders. They both stepped back from the mouth of the cave, as he had not seen them yet. Asmath quickly took Avtandil to a hidden place and whispered a final warning before rushing out.

"You must remain here. None are disobedient to this Knight and live. If God wills, I will soften his heart so the sight of you does not bring his wrath down on both of us."

When she was done speaking, she went out to greet Tariel. As before, when the two met, they embraced in sorrow, sharing a bath of tears between them. Eventually, she removed his saddle and brought it in before returning and helping him out of his armor. When she finished, the two of them came inside and sat together.

Avtandil looked on from his hiding place, wondering what would happen next.

CHAPTER 20

A MAN UNDONE

Though a prisoner now, Avtandil's heart was at last freed from the dungeon of loneliness it had so long been chained in. He looked on in silence as Asmath stretched out the panther skin for the Knight to rest on. When Tariel sat down, he let loose a heavy sigh, morose and brooding. For all his beauty and power, the pain behind his eyes marked him as a broken man.

Yet she, the daughter of patience and forbearance, lit a fire to roast some meat for him. When she finished, she brought him some, but he was too tired to chew and spit the food out. He lay down, turning his back to the world before falling asleep, but sleep gave him no peace.

Before long, he screamed from a nightmare and jumped up in a daze. Like a madman he turned from left to right, chasing unseen spirits. His cries echoed pitifully throughout the cave.

Still in another world, he stumbled over a stone, picking it up and beating his chest with i t while wandering in circles. Asmath screamed at him to stop, scratching her face in horror until her screams reached him. Finally, he hit himself in the head with a piece of firewood until regaining a measure of composure. Horrified at his actions, she yelled at him in fear and concern.

"What happened to you? Why are you so lost as to beat yourself?"

Noticing his blood, he looked up at her with a mix of shame and shock at how far his mind had fled from reason. Sitting back down on the panther skin, he quietly answered her.

"When I left, a King was in the field with his hunting party. The sight of men filled me with sorrow, so I went away from them. I did not want to come near for fear of what I might do, but a man saw me. Pale with shame, I hid in the woods while they searched for me. When dusk approached, they stopped looking, and I returned here. I have no idea how I will continue this hateful existence and cannot think of what to do with myself."

Between sobs, she angrily shouted her answer to his foolishness.

"Look at you, roaming alone in the deepest forests with wild beasts, never seeking a man for help or conversation! There is nothing to entertain you other than the fire in your soul, and it consumes you! How will you ever find her if you waste your days in vain like this?"

"You traveled the whole earth in your quest and crossed over every land. Was no man able to be near you who did not ignite your anger? Were you unable to find a single person to break the tide of your grief and share a moment of brotherhood?"

"If you follow this road alone, you will bring about your death. She whom your heart sings for will be doomed to perish, for none but you can save her. Knowing this, what do you gain from behaving like an animal? How does it help her or you?"

He winced in pain at the truth of her reprimand. Yet, he also understood there was no way forward. All his efforts had failed. No one could lessen his burden, and he did not dare dream of finding a brother amongst the ruins of his life.

"Though you do not lie, your words are sharp against the wound on my soul. No balm or salve on this earth will ease my suffering. Only one road is left to me, which is death. In severing the flesh from my spirit, perhaps I may find some measure of joy. Otherwise, nothing will help me."

"How is it you expect me to find an unborn man? Where would I look for someone who does not exist? More, why would God cause such a man to be on the same world as me? Who did you see other than me with the strength to bear my woes? What man would be so foolish as to attempt helping me with them?"

"Yes, I have become a shadow from carrying this weight. Yet, I found no equal in any other man. Do you think I have not looked? You share my sorrow, but you must also know there is no other in this world who can understand me."

What he said of her words was true, for she did speak harshly, but his judgment of himself was harsher still. He had been over the entirety of the world in his quest, and he knew she was aware of this. Curious as to her line of questioning, he looked long and hard at her. She endured the weight of his gaze as his eyes asked unspoken questions, until she cautiously answered.

"Do not be angry with me or the truth of what I say. Though I speak out of fear for you, what I say is not without wisdom. God appointed me as your advisor, and you have no other. I cannot conceal what is best in this matter. You go to extremes, beating yourself and your soul to no end. In doing this, you overstep the bounds of reason."

Tariel listened, but his frustration grew at not being able to determine the purpose or place of what she was saying.

"Be clear because I do not understand what you want! Do you expect me to create a man without the aid of God? Do not give me half measures of advice and cups of riddles. Rather, tell me what sits on your mind to help release me from this prison."

Asmath was silent for a long time before she spoke again.

"Perhaps I harass you with timidity of speech and too much talking. Yet, I will answer you. If I found a man who would come to you of his own free will and share your burden, would you accept him and swear not to hurt him in any way?"

Tariel laughed when she said this, a mixture of hopeful joy and self-deprecating cynicism in his voice as he answered her.

"If indeed there is a man like this, I would rejoice if you showed him to me. By the heart of her who causes me to wander mad in the fields, I swear to do nothing unpleasing to him. I would love him as a brother and be kind to him for all my days. In me, he will find no cause for bitterness. If one such as he exists in this world, I will do everything in my power to be his friend."

When he finished speaking, she stood, his promise to do no harm still fresh in the air. Walking to him, she laid her hand on his brow and told him to wait. He looked up at her, confused, as she walked behind the towering columns of the cave to Avtandil's hiding place.

CHAPTER 21

AT LAST WE MEET

Asmath came to Avtandil and took his hand, leading him out like a full moon revealed from behind clouds. She brought him to Tariel, who stood and stared at him in wonder. To his eyes, the stranger looked like a star fallen from heaven. Then she spoke, revealing the truth behind her promise.

"In this man, I found the companion you seek."

Looking at one another, the two men understood each had a brother and an equal in the other. Their hearts filled to overflowing, and they were not shameful in their affection, embracing like the moon and sun meeting. With joy, they kissed the other's cheeks, overwhelmed with happiness.

Soon, Tariel invited Avtandil to sit. They sat across from one another, holding hands in silence. Neither knew the tragedy of the other or how to ask. Yet, realizing how torn the spirits of each must be, their own hurt was magnified. They shared grief without speaking until Asmath calmed their forlorn hearts with soothing and beautiful words.

"Do not allow sadness to darken the sun with your eclipse. Calm yourselves, lest you slay one another with your pain. Speak gently, as brothers, and I will attend you as a sister."

Tariel spoke first, curious about his strange new friend.

"You witnessed me earlier, so know already how I am forgotten and abandoned. Because of this, do not ask of me yet, but I would learn who you are. Where did you come from, and where is your home? Why did you come when even death has denied me what I sought?"

Avtandil looked up, deciding there would be no secrets between them, and answered with the eloquence of a Knight.

"You, who are a lion and hero, behave gently towards me. I answer you with joy. For me, I come from distant lands. I am an Arabian in service to the court of King Rostevan. His domain encompasses the entirety of Arabia, but wherever I go, I cannot escape Fate. An unquenchable fire consumes my heart, for I love his daughter, Tinatin. She is King to those who serve her, beloved, wise, and beautiful above all others."

"Though you do not recognize me, I met you many years ago. Do you remember when you brought down the armed servants of Arabia? We found you while roaming the plains, and though we called out, you ignored us. In doing so, you angered my Lord. Because of this, he ordered men to bring you to us, but you left the fields dyed crimson with the blood of our soldiers."

"Without lifting your sword, you split the heads of all who attempted to seize you, striking them with your whip. The King became so angry he mounted and chased you, but you vanished like a Kadj sorcerer. Though the best in our kingdom searched for you, we could not find a single track of where you went. Our servants thought a Devi came to us, for we did not understand how a man might so completely disappear."

"After this, our King became melancholy and full of gloom. His spirits grew dark, though surely you know how the moods of a monarch can be. He sent riders seeking news of you, and many went into far lands to find any word or sign of your passing. Yet, no one found you. In the end, he decided you must be an evil spirit. His temperament returned to normal, but you had not been forgotten."

"Tinatin invited me to speak in private, where God himself blessed me. From the rose of her soul, she gifted me words more precious than the finest jewels, confessing her love for me. She bade me seek you out, saying, 'Today I give you my heart for your heart. Take mine with you, and yours I will keep. Carry it far from the kingdom of Arabia and learn of this strange sun who vanished from us. Whether this Knight is real or a Devi, I trust none other than you to discover. I will wait three years and swear to you, I will accept no husband other than you."

"Can you believe I might live so long away from her smile? Since that time, my soul bleeds without end. So often I threw my hands up to Heaven in dismay, but until now, I met none who knew of you. Wherever I roamed, across strange and stranger lands, I was unable to find you. Not until this past week, though only two months remain of the time she gave me."

"By luck I chanced upon three Kurdish brothers. They spoke with joy of hunting but followed with tales of rude behavior towards you. They wailed with sorrow, for you struck one of them so fiercely as to leave him near death. When they finished speaking, one pointed to the edge of the plains. I looked there and saw you vanishing into the horizon like a setting sun."

"For three days, I followed you but kept my distance. I did not want you to see me lest we come to blows. Indeed, it is thanks only to the wisdom of Asmath we sit now with words rather than swords."

Tariel listened intently throughout Avtandil's tale and remembered the events of his story.

"I remember meeting your retinue on the fields, though long ago. I observed you and your master hunting from afar but was lost to ruin, weeping for she who is my destroyer. There was nothing you might want with me. I could not fathom your desire, for we had nothing in common between us. You took joy in your hunt, mighty and sporting amongst yourselves, while I sat alone, morose, and forlorn. My cheeks were bathed in tears at the thought of her for whom I die each day."

"I only wished to be left with my misery, yet you set your soldiers on me, daring to try taking me by force. This greatly angered me. I thought it more fitting you carry away corpses than capture me. As your men surrounded me, I looked around and noticed your Lord approaching. I pitied his Kingship and did not lay hands on him. Instead, I said nothing and chose to disappear before your eyes."

"This is the gift of my steed. It is as if my warhorse is an invisible spirit at times. Before a man can blink, I can flee what is unpleasant for me. Though, of those Kurdish brothers, I do not think I behaved unjustly, though my prowess did not suit them. They were haughty and overbearing. What they received was well deserved."

"I realize only now how you came to me with good intent, though it pains me to know you suffered all these years. However, the sight of your face brings light to me. You are a brave hero with a face like a moon, and at long last, you found what you seek. Though, to tell the truth, I did not believe I would find another man so abandoned by God as me in all the world. Learning we two are so alike is a bittersweet joy."

CHAPTER 22

PITY THE LOVERS

Surprised at how Tariel spoke to him, Avtandil could not help but laugh. He did not expect his new friend to be so eloquent or pleasant, having witnessed the destruction he was capable of.

"How is it one worthy of praise from the tongues of the wise, finds reason to compliment me? I am no more than a Knight of Arabia and servant to her who holds my heart. What did I do to deserve these words from you, who it seems none can stand against or disobey? To me, you are an image of the sun above, a light from heaven. No misery I suffered or tears I cried can change this."

"Your grace is so great it could make me forget her who my life has been so long dark without. Though the ruby of her lips is preferable to me over anything else, I would sacrifice it a thousand times to serve you until my death. Should you but ask, I will renounce my service to she who carries the cup of my life. This is how deeply you move my spirit."

When he heard Avtandil's affectionate and kind words, Tariel smiled, momentarily forgetting his sorrow.

"It is with pleasure and amazement I hear this from you. Your soul warmed to me, and I wonder what service I did for this attachment. Yet, I think this is the law between men such as us. Lover pities lover. You are separated from the woman you love, as I am severed from my own. But what can I offer to you to justify separation from your heart's desire, and why would I rob you of this?"

"Your journeys have been long and difficult. In service of your lady, you searched years to find me. Surely these endeavors and deeds are worthy of song, and now God has given you what you sought. I am with you and will tell you of my own sorrow, which is the cause of my wandering."

"Though, I am not sure how to begin. The thought of sharing this tragedy sets my soul ablaze. I feel the flames of misery and agony will consume me when I tell this tale. It may be that I will become no more than smoke as the words leave my mouth, but I will do my best to share my woe with you."

His shoulders shook as he spoke, visibly disturbed at the thought of telling his story. He remained silent, inflamed with the difficulty of giving voice to his pain. He turned to Asmath, tears teasing the edges of his dark eyes.

"You have been a sister to me all this time and witnessed my every joy. I am sorry you have spent so many years forced to watch sorrow heaped upon me until the light of hope was extinguished. Quite often, I wondered how you did not understand there is no cure for what ails me. Yet, here sits this Knight you brought to me, and I am burned anew by his tragedy. Truly, I am his debtor for tears."

"I was lost earlier today, asking how I would be able to find what God had not created, and then you showed me this man. My heart is born again as if in the embers of a glowing furnace. Before now, my path was cut off. When I heard of your sacrifices, I felt like a bird caught in a net or a hare bound by the snare. If I do not aid him, nothing will remain of the feasts I once enjoyed, except straw for a bed and an old goat hide to cover me."

"Yet, God is truly merciful, as this moon before me showed now. He gifted me with two blessings. First, my hand will reunite two lovers, which is a joy I have no words for. Second, perhaps his appearance will save me from being lost to the fires which nearly ruined me today."

"Of you, Avtandil, I can say only when a man takes a brother or a sister to himself, he no longer cares for his own death or trouble for their sake. Undeniably, I accept you as my own, giving my life for your life and blood for blood. I believe God must not refuse to save one if it would cause the other to perish."

"Now, I will tell you of my tragedy. For as duty has bound you, it equally compels me. When I am done, you must return to the lady who awaits you and share my story. Perhaps through this action, Heaven will allow my own salvation and that of the woman I die for each day."

"When I speak, dear Asmath, please sit by my side. If I faint, bring water, and bathe me, so my burning heart does not consume this flesh of mine. Should the telling of this tale leave me as a corpse, let the earth cradle me. Bury me in this cave with no other marker than a stone for the man God did not comfort these many years."

With this, he sat down and unbuttoned his shirt, baring his shoulders. He was like a sun hidden behind clouds, without a single ray of light spilling forth. At first, he was unable to open his lips to speak. He clenched and unclenched his jaw but still formed no words until, at last, he drew a long and shuddering breath. Hot and fresh tears burst from his eyes as he cried out in anguish.

"Oh, my beloved! Love of my own but lost to me! I do not know who cut you from me, but I have made fires thousands of times in search of you!"

With slow and halting speech, he began recounting his tale of woe to Avtandil. He did not fight his tears or turn away from them. Instead, he let each fall where it would. Asmath sat beside them, bearing witness to the truth of all Tariel and his beloved suffered.

CHAPTER 23

THE SEVENTH THRONE

"What I share now is not lightly spoken of, so I beg you, listen closely. Melancholy overpowers me at the thought of this tragedy, and the weight of giving voice to these events is such I can barely bring the words to my lips. Streams of tears may pour from my eyes like the blood in my veins, but you must not interrupt me."

"Though you see me now, the ruin I have become is the end of this story. The beginning lies elsewhere, in the Seven Kingdoms of India. I am sure you know, as every man does, of Pharsidan, the sun-faced conqueror who ruled over six of these. He was respected for his wisdom and generosity but was also a fierce warrior who led legions into battle. His foes feared him no differently than peasants fear lions."

"Yet, there existed a seventh Kingdom, where the mere word of their army struck terror in those who stood against them. My father, Sharidan, held this Kingship. Though fearsome, he made war with honor. He slew those who challenged him with skill and never resorted to deceitful or underhanded tactics. Because of this, he was well regarded, though none dared to insult him, openly or in secret. Everyone knew offending him was to invite utter destruction."

"However, he lived freely, careless of Fate. Unlike many who keep the Lordship, he could often be found hunting boldly and making merry without worrying over foe or adversary. This caused his warriors to love and adore him. Yet for all his character, my father hated the solitude of leadership. Whenever he spent time alone, his heart filled with woe."

"One day, he thought to himself, 'I am King Sharidan, well seated in power, and unable to be beaten by any who challenge me. I have conquered everything near me and rule all the way to the frontiers, but I grow lonely and desire the company of an equal. Who better to spend my time with than Pharsidan? I will go to him, and together we will celebrate the might of our Kingdom.' With his mind set, he sent an envoy with a message."

"My father wrote a simple and direct letter, reading, 'My King, India is yours, and it is with pleasure I make myself bold and clear to you. I wish to visit the palace and show the power of my heart! May you receive these tidings and know the glory of my faithful service remains with you!'"

"Pharsidan read my father's message with happiness, and answered, 'I who rule these lands give thanks to God for you, a man equal to myself and a Lord of India. Come to me with haste, and I will honor you like a brother and a parent.'"

"When my father arrived at Pharsidan's palace, they celebrated like no two others in the history of our nation. They sported together and played games until late hours. In time they became the best of friends, and he gave my father another kingdom, appointing him as Amirbar."

In India, the title also confers the role of Amirspasalari. This is a position of absolute power in all matters, except in the overlordship, which only the King holds. No higher honor exists, and I cannot justly compare anything else from another realm with it."

"It is important I emphasize that my father earned this title through his deeds and not because of their friendship. In all things, Pharsidan considered him an equal. He often said no man in the world had an Amirbar such as he. They shared duty, honor, and respect between themselves. In quiet times, they hunted together. When war came, they descended on their enemies like a storm, relentlessly hammering their foes until they won peace."

"Though great men, there was one sorrow they did not

share, which burdened Pharsidan and his sun-like Queen. They had no child, whereas my father had me. Unfortunately, he was not a man familiar with children and was often absent with war and matters of court. My mother died giving birth to me, and though I had an endless stream of nursemaids, I did not know what it was to have a mother or a family. Nor was I aware then of the Kingdom or its problems."

"However, as Amirbar, my father's first duty was securing the country from threats, and this came before anything else. Even his son. The lack of an heir was causing unrest within the armies of India and emboldened border nations. Many worried over the lordship having no children. Seeing the distress of his men, as well as reports of enemies on the frontier, my father acted in a way only he could. To secure the nation, he presented me to the King and Queen as their own child. They rejoiced at having a son to raise, and it gave a measure of peace to us all."

"Yet, I regret that day, for it brought me to where I am now. I am not the same as my father, as none are like me. You will learn this as I tell the story of what came to pass by my hand, but at that time, we were all joyous. My father gave me what he could not provide, and for my part, I learned what family meant."

"Being raised by Pharsidan and his Queen, I wanted for nothing. They cherished and loved me as their own son and made me Lord of all the soldiers and countries. To hone my mind, they appointed scholars to instruct me in the behavior and carriage expected of a ruler. Generals and tacticians taught me the arts of war, and in time I grew wise and strong under their tutelage."

"Asmath can confirm I speak truthfully, but at five years of age, people compared me to an opened rosebud. Fairer than the sun in beauty, I could slay a lion as easily as a sparrow. Pharsidan took such pride in my accomplishments, he forgot he had no son of his own. Those who looked at me said to themselves, 'He is like a nursling of Eden.' But now I am a pale shadow of my former self, though it pains me to recall."

"One day, when I was still only five, the Queen learned she carried a child. When she gave birth, they made a huge celebration to announce the good news of their daughter. Lords and their hosts came from every corner of the Kingdom, and some from the farthest frontiers. They brought exotic gifts and loaded the arms of soldiers with treasures and presents."

"My heart filled with joy. The King and Queen were as father and mother to me and would love us both equally as their children. When I first laid eyes on the new princess, she sparkled with light, like a star. Though the tongue I possess cannot give sufficient praise, I will tell you of her, despite the words consuming me with flame."

He moved his lips to speak more but swooned with dizziness at the thought of mentioning the as-yet unspoken maiden's name. He began to sob uncontrollably. Avtandil held him, his heart burned to soot by the pain his brother carried. Asmath sprinkled water on Tariel to bring him back from the abyss of his sorrow, her own cheeks streaked with tears. At last, he let out a shuddering sigh of agony.

"Truly I say to you, my world is lost. This is the day of my death. It comes upon me as I say her name. She is forever separated from me, and I am ruined by what can never be found."

CHAPTER 24

RISE OF THE PHOENIX

When Tariel returned from the fiery edge of his abyss and calmed himself, he continued the tale, though visibly pained.

"The maiden I speak of was named Nestan-Daredjan, and I wonder how my heart still beats while separated from her. At seven years of age, she was gentle and wise. None in India or the world compared, and the sun was unable to equal her beauty."

"Years passed, and she grew as I did until we both had our own responsibilities. Pharsidan looked to her as heir to the Kingdom and one day sent me home to my father. It hurt me to part from the only family I knew, but I was growing into a man. There were duties I must soon assume, so I continued training in the arts of war and Kingship. When I had time, I played ball on the square or hunted, killing lions with no more effort than if they were cats. However, my greatest joy was being old enough for battle. I could tell you many stories of my early conquests, but they have no place in this tale. Instead, I will return to speaking of the woman I burn for."

"The King crafted a small palace for her, where she might rest comfortably. He used rich bezoar for stone, with cut jacinth and ruby to accent it. Along the corners, alcoves poured incense into the air day and night. In front, they built a walled courtyard so none might look over or around. In the center, they placed a fountain of rose water for bathing, with flowers and songbirds surrounding it. She lived there, sitting in the tower on some days and descending to the shade of her private gardens on others."

"To attend Nestan, Asmath and two other servants were appointed. They would play games together, often enjoying backgammon amongst themselves. For an advisor and tutor, he gave his own sister, a widow named Davar. She previously married in the land of Kadjet'hi to a Kadj, and she would teach the maiden wisdom."

"In addition to the walls around Nestan's palace, curtains of gold and costly fabrics hung over the windows and doors. No one could see from the outside how she grew, but her face became like crystal and rose. In form and shape, she developed like the sacred tree of Gibeon. None compared to her in beauty or grace, nor do any today shine with light as she did."

"In those years, I was a boy of fifteen, having been brought up with two Kings as fathers. When they sent me home, I found almost no time to sleep. I trained each day under the watchful eyes of my father, King Sharidan, and grew in power. Everyone celebrated me, and in particular, my feats of archery."

"I spent time honing and refining my strength of body and mind. None equaled me in the fields or in lectures. On some days, I would hunt the plains, slaying all manner of beasts and game, and then return to play ball in the square. Other times, I was lost in ancient books or learning philosophy and wisdom from old men. As my success grew, I made feasts with friends and became accustomed to continually rejoicing. Yet Fate would sunder me from my joy. I just did not know it then."

"Before long, my father died. While it is true no man is a stranger to sorrow, his loss wounded me deeply. Some suggested I should be thankful for the father I still had in the King, but I do not take advice from fools. What man celebrates the eye remaining when he has lost the other? At first, Pharsidan appeared worse off than me. He gave up all merriment at the news of my father's death. All throughout the Kingdom, those loyal to him mourned my father. Meanwhile, our enemies rejoiced at the passing of one who inspired terror in them. Some went so far as to openly disrespect the rule of India."

"As for me, his death extinguished the light of my world. I sat in the dark, lost and annihilated by Fate. By day and night, I groaned in unending agony. I was a prisoner to the cage sorrow wove around me. At the end of one year, courtiers came to me from Pharsidan. He ordered me drawn out from the darkness I shrouded myself in, and they read his commands to me."

"'Tariel, the time has come to cease your mourning. I lost a brother and would not also lose a son. We grieve equally at the loss of our friend and peer, but you must put away the black you clothe yourself in and come to me.' With this message, he sent a hundred treasures and more, though I barely looked on them, such was my grief."

"Yet, I understood it was time to leave behind what darkened my days and bring myself before him. No doubt you know the will of Kings is not lightly defied, even by a foster son. Pharsidan was no exception to this, and I went to him with haste. The mix of joy and sorrow at our meeting cannot be told, but it lit fires anew within me. He gave me the lands and Lordships my father possessed. More, he appointed me Amirbar, saying, 'Go forth now, and with my blessing, fulfill the duties of your father before you.'"

"How can I explain the emotions this kindled in me? My heart burned with inextinguishable furnaces for the sake of my father. The same men who brought me the letter led me once more into the world of the living. Everyone celebrated my return. People came from all over the Kingdom to meet me, kissing me with kind regard as if they were parents."

"The King and Queen seated me near their thrones, honoring me as their son. Both spoke to me of my obligations and duties to our country. I realized the highest honor I could give the memory of my father was to be like him, so I put my grief away."

"I agreed to their appointment, though had I wanted to deny it, they would not have accepted. As Amirbar, I submitted myself to the responsibilities of my new station, paying homage to my duties. I would serve them and India, and in name and duty, I would behave like my father."

"Many years passed, but there is no point to tell them all. Those times are difficult to relate to, for I am a different man now, and it seems the Fates always do evil anyway.

Besides, there are more important things to tell. What you have heard thus far is only the beginning. Pray for me so I might reach the end of this story before perishing, for sparks from the anvils of my agony burn me even as I speak."

He paused, a shudder escaping him before he fell silent again. Avtandil and Asmath consoled him and tried to soothe his hurts. How much time passed cannot be said, but the three shared sorrow for their own loss and the pain each of them carried. Eventually, Tariel was ready to tell more of his story.

CHAPTER 25

LOVE BURNS

Asmath gave Tariel water, which he sipped slowly before taking a long breath and continuing his tale.

"One day, when I came back from a hunt, Pharsidan came to me and said, 'Come. Let us go and see my daughter Nestan.' Yet, I had not seen her for many years. Our duties kept us from the sight of one another. She grew in her own way as I in mine. Still, he took me by the hand and led me to her."

"We came to the small palace where she lived, and I looked on the garden for the first time. It was fairer than any place of delight I had seen before. There were fountains of rose water and countless birds singing more sweetly than any siren. Slim and tall cypress trees encircled the emerald walls of the courtyard, and gold curtains hung over the entrance."

"The King went in, walking directly to the tower, but I remained behind. I knew he wished none to look upon his daughter. As he entered, I glimpsed what was within. The interior was covered with intricately woven rugs, interspersed by tapestries of the finest gold and silks. On the far side, I saw a curtained canopy, where a sleek spotted panther rested."

"From inside, Pharsidan called me. To my surprise, he ordered me to bring decorative partridges. When I returned with them, he told Asmath to take the birds to the princess as a gift from the Amirbar. Though I could not hear what else they said, when she came out to take them, I caught the briefest glimpse of

Nestan before the curtains fell back."

"How the memory of that day pains me. When I laid eyes on her, a fire was lit in me which burns my soul to this day. I did not know how fiercely love would scorch me. In that moment I began paying my debts to Fate. It was as if a lance of adamant pierced my heart of stone."

"In a daze, I handed the partridges to Asmath. She took them, and I stood before her, wreathed in flames at seeing Nestan. Since then, this burning never stops, though I fear it consumes me to no end, for she is lost!"

As the last words escaped his lips, Tariel collapsed and fell over with a groan. He, a man of such brightness the sun despised him, was unable to speak more. Avtandil and Asmath stood over him, lamenting the wounds he suffered at telling his tale. Their cries echoed throughout the cave.

"Woe is he, laid to waste by the hand of Fate. The might of his arms now no more than straw, though before they brought so many heroes to nothing!"

Asmath sprinkled water on him, and together they watched over the fallen hero until he returned to consciousness. When he woke, sadness overcame him. His heart was bound by melancholy. He did not talk but instead stood and paced. For a long while he found no path back to the world of words and speech, but eventually he sat down again. In frustration he dug his hands in the earth, tilling his pain into the dirt until bitterly moaning as he finally spoke.

"The furrow of my sorrow runs deeper than an abyss. I cannot tell you how these memories hurt me, lest I fall further into ruin and flame. Truly, I praise those sages and philosophers who oppose this world. Those who believe otherwise are fools. They trust in luck and fleeting promises of gifts, yet in the end, none are spared Fate's treachery. But there is more I must say. Listen closely now, for I will speak as long as life remains in me, or until these words consume my soul."

CHAPTER 26

THE WEIGHT OF LOVE

"When Asmath took the partridges to Nestan, I was unable to move. Love struck me so deeply the force of my mind and body fled, leaving no power to my arms or spirit. I fell, collapsing in a faint, and the world became dark to me."

"I heard a chorus of weeping and sorrow when I woke up. Upon opening my eyes, I looked up from the bed I was in and saw a vast chamber. Countless people surrounded me as if my bed were a ship about to depart, and they came to bid me farewell. I did not realize what was happening or where I was."

"The King and Queen stood near, crying over me, and tearing at their hair. Many Mullahs were there as well, some chanting prayers to God and others pleading to Him on my behalf. I realized they thought I was bewitched. They believed Beelzebub had taken hold of my spirit, the evil Prince of Demons and Lord of the trustless Philistines of Ekron."

"I was afraid, for I did not understand why I lay there or what happened. The reason behind my sickness and absence of mind was a mystery to me. When Pharsidan noticed my eyes open, he shouted with joy and embraced me, tearfully asking, 'My son, do you live? Speak but a word to me!' Yet, I was like a madman and could not answer. Fear consumed me as blood rushed to my heart, and once more, my world darkened."

"The greatest teachers of Islam, our Muqris, stood around me with the Mullahs. Each held their Koran, reading and praying. They thought the adversary of mankind had laid me low, he who is most evil, of whose name I dare not speak. Yet, for me, their words were a jumble. Their speech made no sense, as though they raved gibberish. For three days, I lay like this, lifeless and bereft of reason as inextinguishable fires raged and burned through me."

"The state I was in baffled the doctors called to attend me. They did not have answers, asking themselves what manner of sickness afflicted me. None of their medicines worked. After a time, the chief physician decided my ailment was not a medical condition, but rather one of the heart or mind. They thought a melancholy had taken hold of me. For my part, I was unaware of the world I lay in or their diagnoses. Sometimes I would leap up, uttering idle words and shouting like a lunatic before falling back into my daze."

"The Queen was most distraught. Enough tears poured from her eyes to make a sea, but I did not know this. I drifted, neither alive nor dead. Like a lost soul, I wander without knowing where or why and unable to find my way home. Yet on the fourth day, my memories slowly returned and understanding began to come back to me. At first, it was like a small trickle of water, but soon my thoughts became a raging river. I remembered what happened to me, but now feared I might lose the thread by which I still clung to sanity."

"I lamented the predicament I found myself in, praying to the creator for patience. I spoke without reservation to Him from whom all life flows, asking. 'God in Heaven, I beg you, do not abandon me. I pray, give me strength to endure this burden and rise from here. If I stay, the reason for my plight will be revealed to all. Help me reach home, where my secret will be safe.' He answered my prayers, fortifying my wounded heart and mending me enough to leave."

"I sat up, amazing those in attendance around me and filling them with joy. Messengers informed the King and Queen of my recovery. She ran in, tears of happiness streaming down her face, and Pharsidan came behind her with such hurry his head remained uncovered. He gave glory to God for healing me. All others in the chamber thanked Heaven for the miracle of my return to life."

"They sat beside me, one on either side, and brought a soothing broth for me to drink. I sipped it as my strength returned, telling them my heart was stronger now, and I wished to mount a horse. I said my spirit longed for the song of a river running over stones and to see the verdant green of open spaces. So, they called for horses. I mounted one, and my Lord the other. Together we left the palace, riding through the square and towards the edge of town."

"We crossed the fields, and soon made it to my home. Pharsidan accompanied me to the threshold of my house, making certain of my health before departing. For my part, I went into my chambers, but in truth, I felt worse than before. Woe piled upon me, increasing my grief a hundredfold until I thought I would die. I asked myself what more Fate could possibly do to me. Little did I know then what a cruel mistress she is, or what the future would bring."

CHAPTER 27

ANOTHER LOVE

"I sat alone in my room, bathing my cheeks in tears until they changed to the color of a deep and mournful saffron. Ten thousand knives cut my heart to a stream of ribbons, and still more lacerated me from within. My misery had no end, and when the doorkeeper entered my chambers to inform me a man wanted to see me, I did not care. I asked, 'What news does he have? Either this one or another messenger. What difference is it to me?' The answer he gave would not matter, though my duties as Amirbar forced me to address the man."

"I heard the gatekeeper call back, saying the servant of Asmath came. When I asked what he wanted, the man gave me a letter. What I read surprised me so much it diminished the burning in my spirit. The maiden wrote of her love for me, which I could not understand. I harbored no suspicions about her intent, for she was virtuous and honest, but her words filled me with more sorrow. Until then, I dared hope for some word or sign from Nestan."

"While it was beyond me to fathom why she would care for me or how she so boldly declared her feelings, I realized disobedience would offer no respite. If I did not respond, her faith in me would be lost, and she would denounce me. Any kind words or thoughts she had for me would wither like grapes left too long on the vine. So, I wrote an answer befitting a lover, though, in truth, I was not. My love had been stolen by another."

"Many days passed after I gave my response to her, yet they did not lessen the fires in me. I lost interest in matters of court and no longer attended. When the soldiers went to train or sport and play their games, I did not participate. An endless stream of physicians came and went, but they did nothing to ease or succor the source of my woe."

"This is how I began to pay the joys and debts of the world. The twilight of darkness fell upon me, and the roots of my suffering took hold of me anew. Though the best doctors in India came to treat me, none discovered why what consumed me. All blamed it on a condition of my blood. When this news reached the King, he ordered my arm bled, and I said nothing against this treatment. I wanted no one to suspect the truth behind my ailment."

"When the doctors finished, I rested in my bed, though I cannot say how long I lay there. I was lost to melancholy, but at some point, Asmath's servant returned. He came up, and I wondered what the girl found interesting in me. I did not know her, other than our brief meeting at Nestan's palace."

"The man presented me with another letter. I read it and learned she could not wait longer and wanted to be with me. Surprised, I agreed and wrote back to her. In my message, I told her I would not be late in coming, nor hesitant to receive her in my apartments."

"Having sent my response, I asked myself why I chose to endure the pain of those lances which pierced me. I was Amirbar and a King. India was subject to me. Yet, if the common people knew how I felt for Nestan, they would judge me a thousand times and more. I would be cast down in shame, with no welcome in any region I might travel."

"While waiting for her response, I received a messenger from Pharsidan. He wanted the malaise upon me expelled and gave orders for the physicians to bleed me again. Yet it pleased the man to return with the news I had already been bled and was well on my way to healing. More, I ordered him to inform the King I would visit him soon, saying my joy was doubled. Once because I would see him, and again for my health."

CHAPTER 28

FOR HONOR

"When I arrived, the King joyously received me. He prepared an event, and I was seated next to him on a horse, though not my own. I sat without quiver or arms, and beside me, Pharsidan ordered the royal falcons released. They flew up like a storm, and the partridges they hunted shrank with fear. As each falcon returned to his handler, rows of archers formed to take down the remaining birds, and not one escaped. Everyone cheered at their success."

"Then, we came to my home and had a great feast. We honored those from the field and celebrated my return from the dark. Singers and minstrels performed, the notes and melodies of their songs floating among us like the voices of angels. Meanwhile, the King gave gifts of precious and unique stones to all there. None present had any shred of dissatisfaction, save me."

"Despite the smile I hid behind, I could not keep my thoughts from Nestan. Each new thought added fuel to the fires raging in me. When I feared I might burst into flame in front of everyone, I called my friends to me, and we sat down a bit apart from the other guests. My companions were mirthful and joyous, while I was morose. They pushed their joy on me, calling me a spruce tree and inviting me to feast and drink. To hide my misery and grief, I drank and feasted no differently than them, yet a wasteland of sorrow grew inside of me."

"After a time, the head of my house came to me. He whispered of a woman who came to visit me. When I asked for her name, he said he did not know, but she wore veils worth praise from the wise. Though I did not know who she was, I had him invite her to my chambers. Shortly after, I asked leave of those I sat with, promising to return soon."

"When I came to my room, one of my men stood guard at the door. The presence of a woman shamed me, yet I said nothing. Instead, I halted at the threshold, and she came forward, bowing and saying, 'Blessed are they who are worth coming before you!' This surprised me, for who salutes a lover? I thought her behavior must be because she had no idea how to make love. Knowing this about herself, she bowed before me, but later would only sit quietly."

"Still, I was intrigued and entered my rooms. I sat on my sofa, and she came to the edge of the carpet. It seemed she felt unworthy, not daring to come near me, so I asked her directly, 'Why do you wait like this when you came seeking my love?' Yet, she did not speak. I watched, surprised to see her calculating and planning her words."

"Soon, she spoke, looking down as she said, 'This day burns me with shame. You do not realize how it pains me. Indeed, I came here for this purpose, but you are unaware of my heart. While I am happy you did not keep me waiting, I cannot say if I am worthy of this task. It would seem even now the mercy of God fails me."

"Then the maid stood and came to me. She said, 'It is true. I am bashful with you. Though you should not think what you believe of my desire causes this. The boldness with which I came to you is at the command of my mistress. You must forgive me if I anger you, but everything I do is to please her heart.' And with those words, she produced a letter, handing it to me without looking up. After this, she sat herself a bit away from me and said, 'Read this, and you will learn of whom I speak. It is she alone who commanded this meeting."

CHAPTER 29

THE MYSTERIOUS MAIDEN

"I still did not know who this bold maiden was or why she came to me and spoke the way she did. Then, as I took the letter from her hands, understanding hit me like a strike of lightning. What she gave me was from the woman who consumed my heart. I could not believe I held such a gift from God, and I slowly opened it with shaking hands."

"Nestan, my sunbeam, wrote to me, saying, 'Oh lion, do not let your wound appear! I am yours, so why do you die? I despise vain fainting. When you finish reading my words, Asmath will tell you all I would say, but I must ask, what love do you think pitiful falling and dying is?'"

"'Is it not better for you to show deeds of heroism to your beloved? I desired to be your wife long before today, but there was no opportunity to speak with you until now. When I saw you sitting on a litter, deprived of reason, and raving like a madman, I understood you shared my heart's desire. It was your love of me which struck you down.'"

"'But this is not the way of a hero. You should bring honor and glory to India rather than the tear-stained pity you have presented thus far. I am sure you realize the Kingdom of Khataeti owes tribute, yet they show ill will towards us. This cannot be tolerated, least not by you, Amirbar.'"

"'Go to the Khatavians and teach them the manner they should behave. Make battle with them, and in doing this, you will become the hero I wish to look upon. Truthfully, I tell you, this way is better. Why moisten the rose of your cheeks when the sky can do no more than you have done to yourself? Do not weep idly, for I turned your darkness to dawn with only a word. Now it remains for you to turn my dawn into day, so the light of India's glory might shine on us both.'"

"In that moment, I fully understood how boldly Asmath had spoken to me. I realized she was not a timid woman. Instead, her grace and devotion to Nestan compelled her. Of me, how can I tell you of my joy at the hope her tidings gave me? I feared my heart might fail me, for it beat with such intensity my head spun. The crystal of my face and cheeks lit with flame again and shone like the finest cut rubies."

"I looked at the letter for a long time before I answered, writing shortly, 'Oh moon of my soul, there is no heavenly body which can surpass you. Indeed, the sun must dim in your presence. May God never give me anything to compare with you. I feel such joy, as if in a dream, though it is difficult to believe I still live and read these words.'"

"There was nothing else for me to write. My earlier suffering had emptied the spring of my spirit, yet now a torrent of emotion welled up from me. The intensity of it left me unable to contain or direct what I wanted to say. I told Asmath, 'Hear me maiden, for what I would say flees my grasp. I can give no more answer than this. My reason is washed away. How can a man find sustenance in a field at once ruined by drought and renewed with the monsoons?'"

"Yet she carried more wisdom than me, which is why she is here now. She is my only counsel in the ruin I occupy, and her words are fit for Kings. She bade me write more to my beloved, and I continued, 'Oh sun of my life. You are arisen as a light to me. With only this letter, I am revived. Where before I appeared to die, I will faint no more. Instead, I will be at your service. None upon this earth will stand against me in this. Whatever you ask of me, it will be done. Truly I am a liar if I turn away from any task you set before me.'"

"After this, Asmath told me, 'Now you must do as I say, for this is the command of she for whom you burn. If you follow these words, no one will discover the secret of your love until you reveal it. Come to her palace as though visiting me as my lover. In this way, none will suspect the Amirbar of behavior unfitting his station. You will not ruin yourself, or the woman who holds you captive."

"It was wonderful to see such wisdom revealed from Nestan. This brilliant woman who the sun dared not gaze too long on had an intellect becoming a Queen. She was incredible and now opened her home to me. I would sit next to her, whose radiance caused sunlight to seem like shadows, and be blessed with her refined conversation. What can I say to you of this? My desire revealed itself to me in my darkest hour. I could not truthfully tell you whether I stood in Heaven or on earth at that moment."

"I offered Asmath her choice of jewels and gave her a golden chalice, but she refused them all. She told me she was full of gifts and bracelets and not interested in her own enrichment, but only at what service she might do for her lady. I found her more graceful for her refusal of the riches I offered but insisted she take something. After a moment, she chose a large old, jeweled ring. I cannot say why, nor can I tell you where it was from, but it was her choice, and I left her to it. Then, with my gift in her hand, she stood and went back the way she had come."

"For me, what can I say? Light and life filled me. The wicked spears piercing me an hour before no longer caused me pain, and the fires consuming me burned down to a comforting and warm blaze. Joy lit my darkness, and I happily returned to my comrades at the feast. All around me, they drank and joked, enjoying the company of one another, and celebrating my return. Overcome with my own happiness, I distributed gifts amongst those gathered. Our celebration increased, and for the first time in recent memory, I truly enjoyed myself."

CHAPTER 30

WAITING FOR THE SUN

"The following day, I sent a letter to the ruler of the Khatavians. I wrote directly, as befitting my station, telling the King of Khataeti, 'I, Amirbar of India, write to you. You are no doubt aware of King Pharsidan's rule by God's grace. Throughout our Kingdom, every hungry soul who is faithful is given his fill to eat. Likewise, whoever among them chooses disobedience can blame none but himself for what befalls him.'"

"'Brother and Lord, by this letter, we command your presence. No one will be disappointed or embittered by your arrival, and we will welcome you with open arms. Yet should you refuse to come, we will instead come to you. We will not come like thieves in the night but boldly as befits our station. Truthfully, I say, you should come to us, for I would not have you spill your own blood.'"

"With my letter done, I sent it with a messenger and gave myself the freedom to rejoice. There was much merriment and jubilee of my court at this time, and I celebrated with those around me. The fires of my heart had been calmed, and I was no longer bitter towards Fate. She gave me my heart's desire. Yet, as night is opposite to the day, so too did my moods shift. I began to grow angry at the time lost between Nestan and me. I did not receive any sign from her and became like a madman, annoying everyone with my presence."

"First, I thought to roam the fields and plains, but reason soothed my mind. Instead, I feasted with my comrades, though my desire for the woman I loved hobbled my joy. When I had first received news from my beloved, it came to me like a cup full to the brim. Yet, I now had no way to drink without the hand of another. Worse, no answer came from Khataeti, leaving me frustrated on all sides and pacing like a penned stallion in the confines of his stable. I was bitter indeed, at times cursing Fate, who I blessed just days before."

"On one such day, I returned from the King's palace to my chambers, consumed by thoughts of her. I read the letter she gave me again. When I remembered the moment I opened it, my unreasonable woe was kept at bay. On this day, though, an unexpected knock at my door interrupted me."

"A servant whispered to me of Asmath's man looking for me, and I brought him to a private room, where he gave me a sealed parchment. Though short of content, I could barely contain my excitement as I looked over the message. She, whose knife pierced me, commanded my presence. Joy lit my darkness as dawn upon a field of roses. At last, my chains loosened, and I followed her servant without speaking as we made our way to my heart's desire."

"Asmath met me when we entered the walled garden of the palace. It was every bit as beautiful as I remembered, with the trees silent save the occasional call of a nightingale. She smiled before saying, 'It is a joy to meet you again, knowing my hand removed the thorn which before pained you. Come to the rose of your desire. She waits inside, unfaded and unwithered.'"

"She opened the way for me, pulling the heavy gilded curtains to the side as I stepped in. When I laid eyes upon Nestan, my heart stopped. She sat on a throne in a litter adorned with rubies, and she shone with such intensity the jewels around her appeared to be no more than cut glass. Looking into the inky black lakes of her eyes, I came to life once more."

"She rested her gaze on my brow like the touch of a feather, and we stood there for a long time, neither of us speaking. An intimacy hung between us, and our hearts yearned to reach one another like roses towards the sun. For some reason, our words stopped, unspoken at the exact moment before dawn. Each waited for the other to light the sky and awaken the world, yet one could not move without the other."

"After a time, she called Asmath to her side, who returned to me after a moment. She whispered into my ear, saying, 'You must go from here. Your lady is left unable to speak.' Once again, I was burned to soot, but I did as asked. I stood, turning with a bow, and made my way out."

"When I passed through the golden curtains of the entrance, and she within would not hear me, I turned to Asmath and said, 'It is not long since your words of hope healed me. Yet now, my joy is scattered like sands to the wind. She and I said nothing to one another, so what is to become of me? I am more devastated now than before with the pain of parting.'"

"Ever my advisor, Asmath comforted me with her wisdom. She said, 'Do not let the brand on your heart be seen as you leave. Instead, close the terrace of sorrow you occupy. Open the doors of joy in your spirit at seeing her, who your soul sings for. She is ashamed before you and behaves with the dignity expected of a princess.'"

"Those sweet words were music to my ears. I replied, 'Sister, thank you for this balm you have put on my wound. I beg you, do not keep the nightingale within hidden from me. I will joyously receive any news of her. It will help extinguish these flames, lest they separate me from life.'"

"In this manner, we parted. I mounted my horse, the secret of my true purpose yet intact. To those without, we appeared as lovers, having shared our time together. As I made my way home, the sorrow of not speaking weighed heavily on me. When I came to my chambers, sleep eluded me. I lay in my bed, pain dulling the ruby of my cheeks to the bluest indigo. The black of night was preferable to me, for I did not want the dawn to shine on the misery I felt at separation from the rose of my heart."

"In the morning, I woke from a short and unrestful sleep and learned my man was back from Khataeti. He carried two messages from their King, Ramaz. One spoken and the other written to ensure I would not mistake his answer. Though an unusual way to reply, I wanted to know what he would say to me."

"My messenger repeated the words given to him, 'Amir-bar of India, it will be good for you to understand we are not cowards. Neither are our keeps and castles unfortified. I am not aware of who your monarch is for you speak with me in this way, but he is no Lord over my Kingdom.'"

"I sat down and considered what he said, wondering at the sort of man who would dare be so bold and insolent towards me. More, the disrespect he referred to King Pharsidan with was unbelievable. Curious to learn more, I turned my attention to the letter he sent. However, I feared it held little hope for the fool or the Fate his words would bring down on him and his people."

CHAPTER 31

WORDS AND THEIR WEIGHT

"I held the letter a moment before opening it, weighing what was said without words. None of the adornment or formality traditionally accorded between equals was included on or about the paper. Worse, he used plain parchment with no seal. His lack of decorum clearly conveyed an intent to insult. I wondered long at the arrogance and ignorance of such a man."

"After a time, I opened his message, which read, 'I am Ramaz, King of Khataeti. This letter is for you, Tariel, who oversteps himself. Who are you to dare summon me? I am Lord and ruler of many people, and you are barely more than a child! I will hear no more of your words nor look on anything else you send.'"

"At first, I could not believe what he wrote. My message was firm but delivered with diplomacy and tact. More, one so powerful as Pharsidan does not beg the attendance of those who owe tribute. He commands it. To refuse this summons while also being disrespectful marked Ramaz as a fool. For his insults, my hand would be compelled to educate him."

"I stood then, setting his letter aside, and called my Generals to me. They sent orders to the Lords of the frontiers and more within the borders of India. Over the next weeks, commanders and their Knights arrived from near and far, numbering more than the stars in Heaven. Soon, soldiers covered the plains around my fortress Kingdom."

"It pleased me to see how swiftly the armies came when I called. In all my time as Amirbar, there had been no cause for me to call on the combined might of all seven Kingdoms into one place. Yet now they were before me, a testament to our might."

"Pride filled me at the way they presented themselves. Each man stood alert, forming perfect squadrons. They wore the finest Khwarazmian armor, forged in Guldursun-Kala and tempered in water from the Aral Sea. Every one of them was worthy of song, and we would soon be about the business of songs."

"Standing before them, I raised the royal standard, a flag of red and black. It unfurled to its full glory on the wind, and the countless hosts of my warriors cheered. Then, I gave the order to depart for the Kingdom of Khataeti at first light while silently mourning my plight at Fate's evil hand. How would I lead an army without seeing my beloved sun before departing? The long campaign I had yet to embark on yawned wide like a bottomless chasm, and I was bereft of soul."

"Not knowing what else to do, I retired to my chambers and collapsed on the sofa. Sorrow had already defeated me before the first day of war, and I could not stop my sadness. I said to myself, 'Fate rules with a fickle hand. I find no luck or succor from the bite of her blade. Why did she allow me to lay my hand on the rose if I cannot take it?'"

"I sat like this until a young servant came bearing a gift. I was in no mood to receive presents, yet it is rarely the right of those who rule to turn away gifts. I welcomed the youth into my room, surprised when he delivered the most wonderful thing. It was a letter from Asmath. She wrote. 'The sun you long for calls to you. Come! Is it not better to be with her than weep and moan at the deed of Fate?'"

"Her words sang the truth, and I was unable to deny them. Though twilight tugged at the blanket of night, I quickly prepared myself and made little time of the distance between us. Soon I arrived at the palace where my nightingale dwelled. Asmath met me when I entered the garden gates, smiling as she said, Enter, oh Lion of India. The moon awaits you.'"

"As before, she parted the golden curtain which separated me from my heart's desire. I went in, but the riches did not catch my eye. My sole intent was on seeing the woman who summoned me."

"I climbed up every flight of stairs until I reached the terrace. Nestan sat there, bathed in the light of the full moon, and surrounded by shimmering curtains. Though she wore priceless green silks, they meant nothing to my eyes. The wonder of her form drew me in, for she alone in the entirety of the world held majesty for me."

"I came boldly into her room and walked to the edge of the carpet where she sat on cushions brocaded in gems. I had not seen her face yet, but the fires within me lessened at being in her presence. As I waited, she lifted her head. Our eyes met for the briefest of moments, and my world shrank to the depths of her jet eyes."

"She looked down and commanded Asmath, 'Beg our Amirbar to be seated!' At these words, I sat opposite her and gave myself up to joy, forgetting how Fate abused me earlier. Even now, it surprises me I am able to tell you this story while still drawing breath."

"Soon, Nestan spoke again, saying, 'I am aware my silence hurt you the last time we met, though I did not intend to wither you like a flower in the field. I left you doomed to shed water from the narcissus pool of your eyes, but you must understand my reasons. Reservation and bashfulness are necessary towards the Amirbar, and it is to the benefit of a woman to be modest when speaking with a powerful man.'"

"'Yet, I found it worse to be silent and hide the woe of my heart. Though I smiled outwardly, a secret grief gripped me. The message I gave Asmath was true. It pained me to refuse speech, as there were many things I wanted to say. I am sure you appreciate my discretion, for it is the better part of valor, but I did not wish to cause you pain. Now you know why I did not speak when I sat with you before, but this meeting will be different. Tonight, I will bare my soul to you, and I ask you to know me by these vows and oaths. Should I deceive you, may God return me to the earth. More, if I break my promises, I renounce my place in the Nine Heavens.'"

"'When we are done speaking, you must go forth and attack the Khatavians. Gift those traitors the war they invited, for you are Amirbar. This is your duty. I pray you will come back to me joyous and victorious over our enemies, but what of me? What will I do until I can look at you again? How will I keep myself quiet in your absence? I don't want to be left in waiting. Instead, give your heart to me, undivided and forever, and take mine for yourself in its place. Otherwise, I will perish if separated from you.'"

"Unable to believe the words she spoke, I told her, 'This is an unexpected grace from God. No man deserves what you have found me worthy of. The light of your sun fills my darkness, and I glow with your love. I swear to you, I will be yours until the ground reaches up to embrace me and earth covers my face.'"

"We both swore on the Koran, confirming our devotion to one another. When we finished, she said, 'From this day forward, no other will grace my eyes, nor will their words reach my ears. There is only you, and I am yours.'"

"We stayed together after speaking, sharing fruit, and talking of the many things we would do when I returned. Each of us enjoyed the company of the other until it was time for me to depart. We shed tears for one another over the time we would be separated, vowing to meet again on my return. My heart glowed like a star when I rose to leave, illuminated by her rays."

"Though it pained and irritated me to be far from the crystal and ruby of her beauty, she renewed my will to live. However, a war still darkened the road before me, in which I must be victorious. She who I desired most in all the world would not truly be mine until I settled the matter of King Ramaz and the Khatavians."

CHAPTER 32

FIRST IN LAST OUT

"The morning of our march dawned brightly, illuminating the armies before me. The men were arrayed against a backdrop of azure sky, ready and eager to begin. As their leader, and Amirbar of India, I stood before them like a lion. They waited only for my command. Looking across their endless ranks, I saluted before mounting and ordering the trumpets and bugles to be sounded."

"My Knights readied themselves, and foot soldiers opened the way for me. I rode forward, leading a tide of steel behind me. The time had come. We brought war to Khataeti."

"None can accuse us of cowardice as we marched to the borders of our nation. In every town and village, the people celebrated our might and glory. We were heroes to them, off to slay the snake threatening their homes."

"In time, we reached the farthest edges of our country and crossed into the lands of our enemy. From there, we traveled over hills and mountains beyond any road we knew. With no care for path or track, we made our way directly towards the palace of Ramaz."

"We went on this way for weeks. Every time we came to a village or town, the people fled, though we left them untouched. They had done nothing to warrant my ire. Only their King and those who stood with him would suffer my wrath."

"In time, a messenger approached us. He brought priceless gifts of treasure but could not hide his awe at our assembled might. He used a conciliatory tone as he spoke, 'I bear a message from Ramaz, Khan of Khataeti, who regrets his hasty words. We realize too late the wolves of our lands are nothing before the least creature of India, yet you are lions! We beg you to forgive our sins and if by God's grace you would be merciful, hold back your armies. Do not destroy us or bring the Heavens down on our heads.'"

"'My Lord will swear an oath to you and bind our necks. Every castle and city will be delivered to you without the need for war. Our children and possessions will be yours for the taking should you desire. We ask only for your mercy, as it is unwise to ruin those who would serve you. He invites you to come forward with only a few of your Knights, where he will meet you and swear his servitude.'"

"When the man finished, I had him fed and given a place to rest. While he waited, I called my advisors to me. These were wise men who served my father before me, and we discussed how to proceed. They told me, 'The Khataetians cannot be trusted. You are young and do not know this from experience, but we have seen it with our own eyes. They are traitorous, and we believe they plan to betray you to your death.'"

"'We recommend you agree to this meeting but take your bravest heroes with you. Order the soldiers follow a day behind, keeping them informed by messenger. If Ramaz is true to his word, make him swear before God. Yet, if his men carry treachery in their hearts, pour your wrath over them like an ocean.'"

"I was pleased with the advice they gave me and composed a message of my own, which I relayed to the Khataetian, 'I know of your decision, and it is wise. Life is better than death to you and your people, for stone walls will not stop the might of our army. But I will honor your plea and leave my soldiers behind. A handful of Knights will attend me as we march towards you to accept your surrender.'"

"The following day, I selected three hundred of my best men, each of them a hero. With these lions at my side, I rode before the rest of my army, calling out to the men, 'I go before you as is the way of an Amirbar, first in and last out! Wherever I go, you will march behind me over the same fields and follow my track like shadows. Stay close, for I will call if I need your aid.' When I finished speaking, my Knights and I rode away. We traveled for three days until meeting another man."

"This man carried beautiful robes of the finest materials and another message, 'My Khan wishes you to be near him. He said you are mighty and will receive many more gifts than this when you meet him. Before God, I swear to you this is the truth. He hastens to your side.'"

"I answered in kind, bidding him tell the Khan, 'By the will of Heaven, I will do as you command. I come with haste. We will be most tender to one another. I like a son, and you as a father."

"After this, my men and I continued until we came to the edge of a deep forest where we were greeted by more messengers. They brought fine horses as gifts and saluted me as if I already held the Lordship over them. They said, 'Our King desires no more than to see you. He asked us to tell you he left his home this morning and will see you on the fields tomorrow."

"I kept these men with me, treating them as my own. We put up a comfortable tent they could rest in, and I made sure they ate well. They behaved like groomsmen in my camp, resting and relaxing. But of course, you must know no good deed done to an honest man can easily pass from his heart. After a time, one of those men came to me, asking to speak in secret."

"The man bowed before addressing me, 'I owe a great debt to you. Though it is difficult for me to pay, I cannot forsake or forget this duty. Your father raised me to an extent, and the treachery planned for you pains me. My grief would never end if I saw your rose-faced and elegant form as a corpse. Listen carefully now to what they plan.'"

"'The men who accompany me are traitors. They wish to deceive you with vain praise and worthless gestures, yet their words are no more than smoke before a fire. One hundred thousand troops are hidden in one place and thirty thousand in another. This is the reason they urge you to hurry. If you are not careful, grief will embrace you, and the darkness of eternity will be your blanket.'"

"'The Khan will come a little way to meet you, as agreed, showing admiration and respect. But he will secretly be wearing armor. Meanwhile, you will trust his words and oaths, enjoying the lie of his friendship. His soldiers will make smoke and surround you from all sides. In this way, he will strike you with ten thousand men for each one you have. You and your Knights will be overwhelmed and brought to ruin.'"

"Often, I have heard it said there is honor among thieves, but rarely have I found an honest man in their company. This was one such man, and his honesty pleased me. I thanked him, saying, 'If I am not slain by their deceit, I will repay you whatever you desire. Now, go back to your comrades. Do not let them suspect we met. Enjoy this night and celebrate with them. You earned my thanks, and I will not forget what you have done for me.'"

"I told no one what he shared with me. Instead, I kept it a secret, like unspoken gossip. I would act when the time came, but what is meant to be will happen. Fate gives no quarter to men, and in the end, all advice is equal."

"That night, I secretly sent men from our camp to my armies. Though the way was long, I ordered them to march through the night and come up behind us without delay. The mountains and hills would hide them from my initial meeting with Ramaz, but if I needed them, they would arrive at the perfect moment."

"In the morning, I made sure the Khan's messengers were fed, and sent them away with a sweetly composed message, saying, 'I come now with joy to meet you. Soon we will see one another.' When they were gone from sight, my Knights and I broke camp.'"

"We traveled at ease, and I allowed myself to relax. There was no reason to wrestle my conscience. I knew the treachery planned for me. If Fate decided I would die this day, where could I hide in all the world?"

CHAPTER 33

THE THREE HUNDRED

We journeyed for half a day until reaching a tall peak. From there, dust could be seen rising from the distant plains, and we understood King Ramaz was coming. I had planned for this moment and called my Knights to me. Though a trap had been set, I did not doubt in the sharpness of my sword."

"I told the three hundred before me of the evil intent of our foe, 'Brothers, the Khatavians plan treachery for us. Knowing this, why should the power and might of our arms grow weak? Men who die for their Kings ascend to Heaven, as you all know. So, I ask, do we wear these swords for vanity, or are we warriors? Will we hesitate to engage our enemy, or will we meet them like lions? Now, let us prepare ourselves and destroy these treacherous cowards!'"

"With pride and fierce words, I commanded my men to ready themselves for battle. My heroes put on their coats of chain mail, buckling armor on and strapping shoulder pieces into place before checking their weapons. I arrayed them into squadrons, and we rode out to meet the enemy. Each trusted his skill and the prowess of the men beside him to ruin the plans of our adversary."

"We came down the mountain like an avalanche of steel. When the Khatavians noticed our equipment glinting in the sun, they sent a messenger, who told us, 'King Ramaz looks upon your approach with displeasure. Your betrayal is untimely, and we are amazed by your audacity."

"I ordered the man back with a message of my own, barely missing step in our march, 'I know the deceit of your words and actions. What you planned for me will not come to pass. Call your men and come fight me as is our custom. This day I have taken my sword in hand to slay you.'"

"When their man returned, our enemy hastily made fires. The smoke rose in the distance as we approached, and soldiers came from all sides. The ambush they hoped to hide was shown clear as day. I watched as his men advanced, forming into ranks, though thanks to God, they were yet unable to harm me."

"I took a lance in one hand and put on my helmet with the other, eager for the battle to start. My Knights and I rode towards them in a long line as the treacherous armies of Ramaz drew up on either side, seemingly countless. They stood immobile and calm, undisturbed by our presence and sure of their superior numbers."

"When I came near, they looked at me as if I was a madman. Three hundred Heroes swam in a sea of more than a hundred thousand soldiers, but I did not care. My arm was strong, and my will stronger. I rode down our line, cheering the courage of my men, before charging into the main body of the enemy army. My lance pierced a man with such force his horse fell. I left him to bleed onto the plain, forever departing the sun. However, I would not be stopped with one. I loudly praised the fools before me and thanked those who would whet my blade with their blood. Then, I released my fury on them."

"I swooped down like a falcon amongst hapless partridges, making a hill of men and horses as I threw one upon the other. Countless Khataetian soldiers bore down on me, and I sent them spinning away like dragonflies. I destroyed their two forward squadrons by myself as the onslaught of those behind me carried into their ranks and made many a widow."

126

"The ferocity of my blows left none standing where I struck. All around me, the battle raged. Blood spurted from their fallen soldiers like fountains. Everywhere I went, I ruined mean, leaving them hanging like saddlebags from their horses. Though they pressed hard upon us, we were unstoppable. Men fled from me like lambs before a butcher, no matter where I rode."

"Soon, the ground shook beneath us, and the watchmen of our enemy cried out a warning as the sound of my approaching force was heard. Neither mountain nor plain had delayed my army, and the soldiers I commanded to follow had arrived exactly as planned."

"Now the drums of my men thundered defeat to the ears of our enemies. Trumpets blared in such number one might believe the gates of Heaven opened and spilled forth hosts of vengeful angels. Hundreds of thousands of Indian warriors swarmed towards them, the dust of their approach blotting out the sun."

"When our foe realized doom approached, they wailed in fear. Each lamented his fate, begging to be saved from the slaughter we would visit on them. Yet, I did not stop. Treachery knows no quarter, and I gave them no respite."

"Left and right, their ranks broke. They began to run, but we did not let them go. I cut my way to Ramaz and unhorsed him as he fell with a cry. I was on the fallen King in an instant, like a lion taking down an antelope. He drew his sword, and we fought one another until I knocked his blade away and beat him into submission. But I did not kill him. This was not my plan."

"My men shouted and cheered at the sight of my victory, and what was left of the previously ordered Khatavian army began collapsing. They fled in every direction, no differently than water running down the side of a mountain."

"The initial charge of my rear guard had immediately overcome most of the Khataetians. Those who remained were drowned by the tide of Indians swarming over them. This caused the complete collapse of their few remaining ranks. Those few who did not have the wisdom to surrender were quickly overtaken and thrown down, vanquished to a man. When the dust cleared, my troops feasted on the sweet reward of victory for their sleepless nights and hasty march."

"We now held countless prisoners, each terrified of the fate he imagined I would visit upon them. Most were not even wounded, yet they cried and moaned like sick men. It disgusted me to witness soldiers begging and pleading like lambs, but I could not give them the death they deserved. We needed them, for a vassal state without an army is a liability. Though Ramaz showed himself to be a King among fools, he would still serve my purposes."

CHAPTER 34

THE SPOILS OF WAR

"When I finished surveying my victory over the Khataetians, I turned to what must be done next. Though my arm had been wounded in battle, I could not take time to care for my injury. Soldiers and prisoners required my attention first."

"As I began to give orders on the field, men from my army cheered what was left of the three hundred Knights who led the charge with me. Others offered thanks and gratitude for our victory as I passed them. When I reached our tents, the advisors and Lords who had raised and trained me wept with joy over my success. All who witnessed the carnage my sword wreaked on the enemies of India stood in awe."

"For myself, I felt proud. The plains were colored with the blood of those who sought to betray me to my death. More importantly, we did not fight at the gates of the city. Instead, I seized the entirety of Khataeti without a prolonged battle. In one day, I accomplished what might otherwise take months to accomplish. Yet, I needed to do more, for victory is the smallest part of any war."

"First, I sent my soldiers to collect any riches they could, and they did not disappoint. They returned with smiles etched across their tired faces, loaded with all manner of treasure and jewels. I laughed when I saw this and gave them leave to keep whatever they wanted from the loot. My eyes were fixed on a bigger prize."

"Having taken care of my men's morale, I was free to focus on Ramaz. My councilors brought him to me, and I spoke shortly and directly to him, 'I am not accustomed to suffering evil men or fools. Your treachery warrants death, but I would not cause more innocent blood to spill with the loss of your head. If you drop the fortifications of your cities and turn them over to me, I will allow you to live so you may seek forgiveness for your wrongs. Should you refuse, I will not overlook your guilt, and you will be separated from your head.'"

"Though he was an idiot, I had bested him in battle. When any two people pit themselves against one another, each learns the mettle of the other. Because of this, I knew he was cowardly, and cowards are loathe to part with their lives."

"The offer barely left my lips before he accepted, 'I am ruined by you. There is no power in me to contest your victory. My Kingdom and all within are yours to do with what you will. Bring a Lord who remains faithful to me, and I will send him to our stewards. We will give Khataeti to you.'"

"I brought every one of his Lords to him from our prisoners and let him choose one. My Knights escorted this man to the fortresses of those who remained loyal to the treacherous King, and after several days the governors of towns and cities began presenting themselves to me. They gave us their strongholds, each bringing an endless stream of treasures with their submission. The men and women who ruled repented the folly of their actions and the war they invited, swearing allegiance to me."

"Once I held the entirety of the Kingdom, I traveled across the country to inspect the lands. At every township and castle, they presented me with the keys to their Kingdoms. In time I visited everywhere except the palace."

"Wherever I went, I calmed the people, telling them, 'Do not fear me. I did not come to destroy you or your homes. Though I shine like the sun, I will not burn you, nor will I harm you. My actions are the reason your cities and castles fell without war or bloodshed on the citizens. Continue your lives in peace, and I will not disturb you.'"

"At last, I came to King Ramaz's palace. I was unable to believe the treasure amassed there. You would grow tired of listening to me before I described them all. Yet, one item stood out above everything. It was a beautiful cloak and veil, but nothing I knew of could be compared with it. The fabric was woven in a strange foreign pattern and made of some material I had never seen."

"Everyone marveled at the workmanship, but no one could tell me what it was or where it came from. I learned it was immune to fire and strong as steel despite being thin and light as a feather. Many claimed it to be a divine miracle, and I found no reason to doubt this."

"I put this wondrous item together with a number of unique and precious gifts I thought Nestan would like. For Pharsidan, I chose the best items from each of the countless treasuries. When I finished gathering everything, we needed a thousand strong mules and camels to carry it all. Before they left, I sent a letter ahead sharing the good news of our victory."

"I wrote, 'My Lord and father, fortune smiles on us. The Khatavians plotted treachery, planning to ambush us and slay me with trickery, but they failed. Unfortunately, this deceit delayed word of my success. However, I captured their King and bring him to you now. The road will be long, for we have many prisoners and carry much treasure. I will rejoice to see you on my return to India.'"

CHAPTER 35

ENEMY MINE

"After I sent my letter to Pharsidan, I appointed advisors and generals to remain behind and oversee the affairs of Khataeti in my absence. Then I set out for India. Though Ramaz was my prisoner on the long journey home, I treated him as an equal. For me, I held everything I wanted in my hand. I was flush with wealth of every kind, yet glory and honor were the currencies I cared most for."

"In time, we made our way to the palace of my King. He met me like a father to his beloved son, giving me praises I cannot lightly repeat. When he noticed my wound, he changed the dressing himself, wrapping my arm with fresh and soft bandages."

"Soon, a great celebration was held for us in large tents they had placed in the square. I rested there with my Knights for all to gaze upon. Many people came to praise us, and especially me. Others brought fine gifts and succulent delights, which we consumed with joy. Pharsidan sat beside me, looking on with love in his heart. We spent the evening feasting and celebrating together with those came to adore us. My happiness was boundless at being home and in the company of my people."

"In the morning, we left for the halls of justice, having enjoyed the night until the first rays of the sun graced us. The King sat in the chair of judgment and commanded the Khatavian prisoners to be led in one at a time. He questioned each and judged them according to their worth until only Ramaz remained."

"I brought the traitor in myself, for it was I who bested him. Despite his betrayal, I showed him every respect. He came with humility, and Pharsidan gazed on him sweetly, as one might look upon a son he once cradled. This gesture alone made it appear as if the deceitful one deserved such affection. For this is the truth of heroism. The brave show compassion to those they overcome, even the undeserving."

"My King caressed him, and they spoke together until morning, when he summoned me. With a soft voice, he asked, 'What do you say, my son Tariel? Should I forgive the Khatavian, an enemy just moments ago? Is it fit for me to restore the trust he so treacherously severed?'"

"I thought about what my Lord said, and after a moment, I answered him truthfully, 'It is the will and action of God for sinners to be forgiven their trespasses. Because of this, we must also be merciful towards those who brought themselves to ruin with sin.'"

"King Pharsidan stared at Ramaz, and the steel of his will could be seen behind the diplomacy he showed the captured Khatavian, 'You betrayed me and those I love, but it is my hand which sends you from here with forgiveness. Though, I wonder, would you be so considerate towards me if I were in your place?'"

"'Think about this on your road home, for today you have witnessed my compassion. I do not send you away bare headed with empty hands and a broken crown. But know this, if you dare show yourself before me in disgrace again, you will learn the weight of my wrath.'"

"When he finished speaking, he gifted Ramaz a tribute of ten thousand drachmas, all in Khatavian money. Then he dressed the defeated Khan and his courtiers in finery, giving them silk brocades and satins before sending them away. Such was the mercy and wisdom of Pharsidan that even a traitor might win a pardon in place of the punishment he rightfully deserved."

"On hearing his reprieve, Ramaz bowed low before the King. He thanked him profusely, paying homage and saying, 'Let it be known before God, I repent the treachery I once planned towards you. If I sin against you again, it falls to your hand to kill me.'"

"Pharsidan nodded at his words, dismissing him and his men and returning the other prisoners to the Khatavians. Once their retinue gathered in full, they made their way from the palace without insult or injury, preparing for the long journey back to Khataeti. The actions of my King had demonstrated his superiority to all."

"By the time our shamed enemies finally departed, my power was spent. The wound I received in battle throbbed, and no spirit remained in me for the necessities of court. It pleased me to witness the compassion with which my Lord ruled, but I craved rest. When the last of our affairs finished, I retired to my chambers, thoughts of Nestan close to my heart, though I still had not seen her for whom my soul sang."

CHAPTER 36

ONE HUNDRED KEYS

"A man from Pharsidan woke me at dawn with a message, 'My son, I know you desire rest, but you were away for three months. In all this time I have not hunted or eaten game killed in the fields. If you are not too tired, come to the audience hall. I await you.'"

"Though I was weary, one does not lightly refuse the summons of a King. So, I dressed and made my way to him, where I met packs of hounds outside. As I entered, I was surprised to see the chamber filled with birds of prey and him sitting in the middle of them. He wore hunting finery and shone like the sun. When he saw me, he clapped his hands with glee, laughing and rejoicing at my arrival."

"I did not know it then, but earlier, he had he met the Queen in secret before inviting me. There, he shared a plan with her, 'When I gaze on our hero returned from war, my heart sings. He should be seen by all in this way. It brings light to those around him, however dark their hearts.'"

"'Whatever I ask of you this day, do it without delay. Though I made this decision without your consultation, you are a part of it. Our Nestan will one day rule, and today she will be seated beside you. So, wherever you are when I return with Tariel, you must both come to meet us. We will be full of joy from the hunt, and he will rest his eyes upon her.'"

"Unaware of their plans, I only saw a hunting party arrayed before me with my King at the ready. I joined him, happy to be home in India. We left with our hounds in tow, followed by countless falcons and hawks. The two of us hunted over the plains, crossing over foothills and up small mountains in our pursuit of game."

"We returned before sunset, carrying the bounty of our hunt. The people were joyous when they saw us, still flush with news of my victory over the Khatavians. Men playing ball stopped, dropping their games unfinished to laud us with praise and share their happiness at my return. The city overflowed with people cheering, and they spilled out from the bazaars and onto rooftops to see me."

"I wore tasseled robes, with the veil and cloak I found in Khataeti. To our onlookers, I appeared as a pale-hued rose, bathed by the tears of an angel. All who saw me swooned. Those whose hearts I drove mad with adoration became more maddened. Every step went on like this until we reached the palace."

"Once there, the King dismounted and invited me into his private apartments. When I stepped into the banquet hall, my breath was taken. There she stood, the desire of my every waking moment. Her cheeks sparkled like sunlight, blinding my eyes, and leaving me trembling. I did not expect to see her here. Especially not in front of her father, who normally kept her hidden from all eyes."

"Yet she was here and real, clad in brilliant orange and shining like a rose. Her spirit illuminated the room, and I could imagine the light from her spilling into the streets like a sun. She showed the briefest of smiles, but I was dumbstruck and could do no more than stand there, my wounded arm hanging useless in its sling."

"Then, the Queen came to meet me, tenderly kissing my cheek as a mother kisses her son. She loved me, as did my foster father. Their boldness in the presence of the assembled people and Nestan brought both surprise and joy to me. She turned and addressed the people gathered in the hall, 'The Amirbar returns victorious. From this day, we can expect no foe to challenge him further.'"

"The guests applauded, heaping praise on me, and she seated me opposite her for whom I was slain. My seat pleased me, for I could secretly watch Nestan. Throughout the evening, I stealthily stole glances at her, and she to me. While we exchanged many a look, there was no conversation between us. Every time the ceremony required me to tear my eyes from hers, my heart died a little."

"Yet, all around us, people celebrated and shared their merriment. Tables were set with goblets and cups crafted from ruby and turquoise, next to jeweled golden plates worth a Kingdom each. Wine flowed like a river, and Pharsidan invited those who might drink too much to stay and enjoy the hospitality of the palace apartments. Everyone feasted with him and his Queen as though they were all equally Lords."

"I gave myself up to the joy surrounding me, though I could not long keep my eyes from the flower of my soul. The pleasantry of being face to face with her after so long overwhelmed me. I became wild to see her, and whenever she returned my gaze, the fires in me stilled. Yet, I feared to stare too long or obviously. I did not want my affection for her to be noticed."

"After several hours, the King ordered the minstrels to cease singing. They bowed their heads in silence, and he turned to me, 'Tariel, my son, I cannot tell you how we rejoice at your return. It is a bliss to be with you again. Meanwhile, our enemies are filled with woe at the folly of their ill-conceived challenge.'"

"'Many are the men and women in these halls who rightfully are your admirers. They do not sing your praises idly. It is the truth they speak, and we too would honor you. As is custom, we will clothe you to match the might and glory of your deeds, though we will not take away the beautiful robes you wear now.'"

"'Instead, you who light our lives with the fire of your Heavenly rays will receive a gift from our hands. In this way, you may order whatever you desire sewn. Do not be bashful, for your victory is ours too, son of India!'"

"They handed me the fabled one hundred keys, which everyone knows lock away indescribable treasures. Empires would blush at the hoard of wealth this gifted me. I gave blessings beyond counting for their generosity, and they rose, kissing me tenderly. Each of them was shining, like two suns come down to illuminate me. At no time had anyone honored me as much as they did that day. Nor did any army see gifts equal to those I would later present my soldiers from the treasure I received."

"The King and his Queen took their seats once more, joy radiating from them like sunlit cherry blossoms. All around us, the singing and drinking increased. The gentle melody of lyre and tinkling of harps soothed and caressed us as we feasted. When the kiss of dawn tugged at the edges of the sky, our Queen retired to her rooms. However, many of us remained and continued celebrating, though our joy was lessened by her absence."

"When evening came, the feast finally defeated me. I could drink no more double goblets of wine and took my leave, paying my respects as I left. When I made it to my chambers, I fell to my couches like a man dazed, rejoicing at the memory of being so long under the raven lashes her who I so loved. My heart and body were still her prisoners, but I had no power to extinguish the fires which consumed me."

"As I rested my head, a servant came to my door with news of a veiled woman waiting for me. I understood at once who was there and ordered him to let her in. Asmath came through my door with the elegance of an angel, and I kissed her on the forehead. I took her hands and stopped her from bowing, seating her near me on the couch as I greeted her, 'You are a blessing to me, like a new shoot from a spruce tree, filling me with wonder and joy. Tell me of her who has slain me with her eyes, and nothing else.'"

"She smiled, pleased to visit me and share the words of her mistress, 'Do not think I came for no purpose other idle chatter. I watched your pleasure these days at the tender sight of one another and come at her command to give you more than news, as you will learn now.'"

CHAPTER 37

I HOLD YOU WITH ME

"Asmath drew a letter from beneath her robes, and I took the paper from her hands. What I held came from the light of my life and I gazed long upon it. Then I opened it and read the elegant words my love had written me."

"'If I died from missing you, I would not be able to share my thoughts. You must hear them now, though they are bold. I hope you can forgive me, but as God gave me this tongue, I will use it in praise of you.'"

"'Having seen the loveliness of your gem-like brilliance in the palace, I am certain my tears did not flow in vain. I am thankful you urged your horse home so quickly, for I enjoyed looking on you freshly returned from battle. You are fair to my eyes. Put your grief away and weep no more from this day.'"

"'While you were gone, the sun made a garden of rose and jet for you, which resides in my heart. My soul belongs to none other than you. Now, give me the veil you wore today, so I may keep it as my own. You will see me wearing what was yours, and I will feel as if you hold me. In turn, I will give you this armlet, which is my favorite above all things I own. Bind it around yourself and cherish it as you love me. This way, you will never spend another night wholly separated from me.'"

"'You will have what is mine, and I will rest safely wrapped within what is yours. Together we will hold one another, no matter how far apart. Know too, there will be those who look on you and curse whoever looks on me, but do not let them disturb you. Lions do not concern themselves with the desires of scavengers.'"

Tariel stopped speaking then and took something from his arm before pressing it to his lips. Then, he held it out to Avtandil, who could not believe his eyes. He was looking at the armlet of Nestan. It seemed to be made from a stream of woven gold. Jewels appeared to move in and out of it, shifting and shining with multicolored hues.

Asmath wept as she reached out and closed Tariel's hands over the armlet. He choked back sobs as she did so, and she embraced him, stroking his hair, and speaking soothing words through her tears. He shuddered with the effort of maintaining his composure, and after a moment, spoke again.

"I still live, though the earth drinks of my blood, yet I am fortunate to find myself in the company of friends unmet. The one joy remaining to me is seeing your face. Though I behave like a madman, you did not abandon me. You sit beside me in this cave, listening to my woe. Perhaps I am not so abandoned by Fate as I think. I will continue this tale of the woman who I am buried for."

"I told you of the gift given to me, but I had something of my own to give. I immediately removed the strange and mysterious dark veil and cloak I wore and handed it to Asmath. After, I wrote a letter, saying the words I now recite to you."

"'Your first words were like an elixir to me, lifting me from the depths of the darkness I suffered in your absence. The rays which shine from you strike me deeply. For all my prowess in battle, I am brought to nothing before your beauty. What service can I offer in exchange for the life your love restored to me?'"

"'Your hand released me from a prison no other was able to open. Your armlet is now with me, and my spirit soars like a falcon. As I gave my heart, so do I hope you will receive this veil. More, I will gift you a cloak of the same strange material, for you also keep my soul. In all the world, you will find nothing finer or rarer than this. Nor will you find a love equal to mine. But I beg you, do not leave me alone these days, for who else can I submit to?'"

"I gave Asmath my letter when I finished, along with the veil and cloak. She rose from her seat and gracefully left my chambers. For me, I caressed the bracelet Nestan gave me and fell into a pleasant sleep. Later, I found her in my dreams but awoke to find her not with me. When I could not find my way back to the dream, I lay awake, thinking of her."

"Though her voice and touch were still on me, it was no comfort. I passed the night holding my hand around the armlet and lamenting the burden of life without her beside me."

CHAPTER 38

NESTAN'S WEDDING

"In the morning, before the first light of dawn, I awoke to voices outside my chambers. I rose to find my servant, who told me the King and Queen wished to see me. Concerned at what might cause them to call me at such an early hour, I dressed and immediately made my way to the palace."

"When I arrived, they were waiting for me with three of their most trusted advisors. I was invited in and asked to sit as they spoke, 'God has brought old age upon us. Our youth is past, no differently than seasons fading throughout the year. The burden of ruling has exhausted us, yet we have no one to assume the throne in our absence. Raising you, we never wanted a son, but now there is no one left to rule.'"

"'We can marry Nestan to someone, but as of now, we have no husband for her and do not know where we can find a man worthy. It must be someone to whom we can entrust our Kingdom to, who would be our own and formed in our image. One we can trust to sit beside her and guard the realm. Do you have any idea can we find such a man, who would ensure victory over our foes, and keep the swords of our enemies from us?'"

"Their words cut me in ways I didn't know I could be hurt. I had always considered them as my family, but what they said left me in disbelief, 'Though I agree Nestan is enough to carry our hopes, how can your heart not feel the want of your own son? My first duty is to India, so I must support whatever decision you take, but what more can I say? How can I offer you advice in this matter?

Surely you know what is best for the Kingdom. I am certain whichever man you choose will rejoice at his good fortune.'"

"How they hurt me. But what could I say? From what they said, in their eyes I was neither suited to marry my love, nor as a son and heir. So, I sat mostly in silence as they began to discuss how to proceed, believing nothing I might do or say would change their minds. Knowing this, I did my best to steel myself and stop the flames in my heart from burning me to soot. How it pained me to be a part of the counsel to my own ruin."

"At one point, Pharsidan spoke, saying, 'I know of a man in the Persian Kingdom of Khvarazma, the son of King Khvarazmsha. None are like him. He is a lion, fierce and proud, commanding a vast host of armies. If this Lord would give us his child for ours, our worries will be gone.'"

"Here, to my eternal pain, the Queen spoke up, saying, 'It is true. He is mighty and known far and wide for his benevolent rule and military prowess. Surely this youth is worthy of our daughter! Who else would be a better choice as our son-in-law?'"

"To say I died at this moment is to compare the sun to a candle. I understood at once they had discussed the matter between themselves earlier. They were guarded as though holding some secret from the rest of us. Though I wished to speak against this injustice, it was not my place to do so. Instead, duty forced me to agree with their decision. Nothing I could say would hinder what they both clearly desired. I burned to cinders and fell to ash as the day of my ruin was set, and Fate once more pressed her black hand down upon my soul."

"The King and Queen sent word to Khvarazmsha, asking for his son. They wrote, 'The throne of India is left without an heir, and in the entire Kingdom, only one daughter of royalty remains. She is fit for childbearing but not to be wed abroad. Instead, she will remain here with whomever she marries. Yet if you would agree to our terms, we will give her hand to your son. Come quickly, and we will gladly receive you.'"

"They loaded their messengers with gifts of rich cloaks and veils of the finest silks, and they were not disappointed with their efforts. Khvarazmsha rejoiced at their coming and gave

Pharsidan and his Queen a joyous answer, writing, 'By the grace of God, we have what we wanted most. No other child in the world can be compared with yours. Who else is better? Our joy will be immeasurable in marrying our son to your daughter.'"

"I was ordered to prepare men who would bring the Persian prince into out palace, so he could steal the jewel of life from me. I had no words for what I felt. Duty required me to remain Amirbar while a foreign man invaded the Kingdom I was bound to protect and stole the woman I gave my soul to. Not a ray of light fell on me when I realized what cruel designs Fate devised."

"I tried to find mental and physical oblivion by exhausting myself in training, but I could not find peace. In time I gave up and went to my chambers. My hope was to rest or at least seek respite from the mausoleum of my heart, but no salve could heal the wound I now bore. I began enduring pain like nothing I experienced. How I might go on living was beyond me."

"Alone and a stranger to myself, I contemplated the knife of melancholy poised above me. I believed nothing might compel me to live further, but someone came to my door. I bid the man in without concern for him or what message he carried, but after a moment, I recognized him. He served Asmath, and I stood to receive the letter he brought. In it, I learned Nestan commanded me to appear before her without delay."

"When I understood she wished to speak with me, a spark of hope lit within my breast. I did not think I would see her again, as her father had already decided the matter. Yet now she called to me. Filled with new resolve, I mounted my steed and quickly left, making haste to the little garden outside her tower."

"When I arrived, Asmath was waiting, but I could see she had been weeping. Tears still stained her cheeks, and it made me sad to realize my coming caused her grief. I jumped from my horse and came to her, worried at what brought her such woe."

"A frown was etched across her face, and she turned from me without a word, raising the golden curtains and beckoning me into the jeweled tower. Her silence added fresh wounds and worry to my bleeding heart, for I did not know what waited within."

CHAPTER 39

A WOMAN SCORNED

"I followed, afraid of what I might find until I saw Nestan. Relief flooded every fiber of my being at seeing she was safe, but her light did not melt my heart as it had before. She was no longer a full moon to shine on me. Instead, her eyes were darkened with rage, and she indicated I should seat myself far from her, unlike when we last met."

"The veils I gave her were carelessly draped about her head and shoulders, and while she wore the same radiant green silks as when I first saw her, they were stained with tears. Her face was lit with lightning instead of the sun I had come to love, flashing dangerously when she looked at me. The maiden I hoped to meet had become a panther, perched on the edge of a rock and ready to strike."

"Her brows furrowed, and she stared me down with barely contained fury. Her voice stung like whips from a nettle when she spoke, striking me to the core of my being. 'I marvel at the audacity you show to dare come before me. You are forsworn, a fickle and faithless breaker of oaths. Your words are like smoke, but the highest in Heaven will reward you justly for the sins you visited upon me!'"

"What she said left me lost as a puppy before an angry master. I had no idea what I did or how to make amends for it. Her anger was visible and palpable to me, hitting me like a fist, but I pleaded with her. 'How can I answer if I am unaware of the

crime you accuse me of? What did I do other than to be senseless and pale at the absence of you from my life? Where have I
sinned against you?'"

"Yet, as every man knows, a woman aflame rarely hears
reason, particularly from the man who invited her ire. She would
not listen. Instead, she drove the point of her words deeper into
my soul. 'What can I say to one as false and treacherous as you?
I am a fool to let myself be tricked by a man with no honor! You
made me no better than a camp girl, swooning at your mighty
arms while your tongue curried favor and spewed lies to ill ends.
I burn with flame at the injustice you did to me!'"

"'You knew my father intended to bring the son of Khvarazmsha to wed me and did nothing! Instead, you sat with
them as a counselor and gave assent to this treachery! You cast
aside the bindings of the oath you swore to me like some fool
of a soldier with a village maid! I beg to God I might visit ruin
upon you for the cunning you deceived me with and destroy you
and all you love!'"

"Then she began shouting at me, and a thousand tears
streamed down the rose of her cheeks. I felt my heart turning to
stone so I might avoid further hurt, but she finished me before it
was fully hardened. 'Remember when you sighed and swooned
over me? Did you forget how your eyes bathed the fields of India, and from across the entire Kingdom, the finest physicians
and surgeons brought medicines to revive you? I have not forgotten! Yet, you are no different than any other man. Your falsehood will be remembered forever, no differently than how Eve
betrayed Adam. You are filth before me, and since you denied
me, I also renounce you. Let us learn who will be more hurt between us when I finish with you!'"

"Her blow left my sword arm weak as that of a child holding a toy. I had no defense from the cuts she laid on me, and I
understood then why sages say hell hath no fury like a woman
scorned. But she was not done. Her fire was far from spent."

"Like Achilles dragging the body of Hector, my death
would not satisfy her. She continued piercing my ruined heart
until no more than a shadow remained of me. 'You made a grave
error in betraying me, and like the lie of your words, you will

be judged by me. So long as I live, I swear by God, you will not find a home here, for I will rule beside whoever rules! Wherever you go, you will find no other like me. However much you reach your hands up and beg to Heaven, they will be left empty! If by some chance you are too cowardly to leave and choose to stay, I will watch the soul separated from your body.'"

"My spirit wilted as her tongue flayed the skin from me. Better I stood against an endless legion of heroes than suffer such pain. Had Ramaz and his armies faced her wrath, not a blade of grass would remain standing in all of Khataeti."

"But there was truth to what she said, no different than there are needles in every haystack for the men willing to find them. She did not discard me out of hand, but instead believed I willingly turned her over to wed to the son of Khvarazmsha. Knowing this, hope revived a few shreds of my heart. I found enough power in myself to look once more on the light of her whom I loved above all else in the world."

"Though Fate has often laid her hands on me to drain the blood of my life and take my breath, this was not to be her day. Do you not wonder how I survived the lance of those words she so artfully threw into me? It was faith alone which enabled me to hold my head up."

"Her Koran lay open on the table next to her. I walked over and placed my hand on the pages as I spoke. 'I lack the means to say how you have burned me today. In truth, the sun sets upon my soul, and my spirit departs. Though, as you stopped short of slaying me outright, I will give you an answer.'"

"With my hand still on the Holy Book, I continued speaking. 'If what I say to you is false or laced with cunning, I beg God to bring the skies down on me. I ask to spend my days in ruin and woe, with all the lights of Heaven turned against me. Yet, if you consider me worthy of judgment, hear my words, for I did nothing to visit this harm or hurt on you.'"

"Nestan looked at where I rested my hand, lifting her eyes to mine. When I finished, she spoke shortly, still questioning me and my intent. 'If this is true, tell me why I am led to believe this falsehood? Why would you forsake me to another?'"

"Like a soldier left for dead, I bound and stitched my own wounds, and gave her what she asked of me. 'The arrangement with the son of Khvarazmsha is not my doing. Your mother and father summoned me to court at dawn. They were in counsel with three advisors and asked me to sit with them Yet, it became clear to me they already decided to appoint him as your husband. There was nothing for me to oppose, for no man can stop the will of Pharsidan. I would have been a fool for my pains and was forced to agree with them. What else could I do? I fortified my heart, not knowing how I might survive if you were lost to me.'"

"'My love for you and yours towards me is still unknown to the King and Queen. In their minds, they did what is best for the Kingdom, for they do not realize I will not leave it masterless. I cannot say who is wrong or right in this, but I alone am the owner of India. No other man has any right than me. While I have not met this Prince who comes here, I will never hand the rule of my country to him or Persia. Yet, I am unable to change the minds of our rulers and have found no way to undo what has been decreed.'"

CHAPTER 40

CROSSING THE LINE

"When I finished speaking, I put my hands up in defeat, unsure of what else I might add to what I already told her. Then, I shared the truth of my mind over the last few days. 'I am like a wild beast, and a multitude of thoughts assails me. I readied myself to take you away from here a thousand times and fly across the fields, but what life would that be for you? At the same time, I cannot give you to another man and still draw breath. Then I wonder why you should not take me instead, but as Amirbar, I will not ask you to disobey your father.'"

"'I feel as though my soul is sold a piece at a time for the sake of my heart. The tower of my strength has been turned into a marketplace selling my honor, and I do not know what to do about it. I am unable to confront my King or refuse his will, and neither can you, but I would not be away from you for any reason. India belongs to us. It is our Kingdom, though it appears this is not the will of Pharsidan. I am not sure what we should do or how we can go forward.'"

"Then, Nestan's manner softened. Rain no longer burned her cheeks, and the lightning fled from her eyes. The pearl of her teeth caressed the rose of her lips as she smiled. 'Why is it I too feel you are right in this?'"

"She was silent for a time, thinking, and her voice sweetened as she spoke. 'I am sorry to wound you with my anger.

You are not faithless or treacherous. Yet I found no way to reconcile your earlier words with your actions in my father's court. I thought perhaps you counseled this marriage to the son of Khvarazmsha. It pained me near to death to consider you might do such a thing.'"

"'I know you do not deny God. You give thanks and show faith to the ruler of the Heavens, as you are faithful to me. I beg Him for our good fortune and hope He will allow us to rule together, celebrating our Lordship with joy and happiness. To me, the best of all matches for you and me to be sovereigns, but I do not yet understand how we might achieve this.'"

"Her wrath was spent, and I lay shipwrecked on the shores of her heart. Once more, she became tender towards me. I looked at her face, unable to decide if I gazed at a soft sun or the full moon. She stroked my hair and soothed my wounds. We talked at length, each enjoying the nearness of the other. For a time, we forgot everything around us, content with no more than the comfort of one another."

"After many hours, our conversation turned towards what we could do to stop the planned marriage, and Nestan spoke. 'Those who are prudent never act in haste. Instead, they create the outcome they desire, remaining calm in the face of the storm. We must be like this and put the motion of the world to work for us. If we plan our course together, we will grind our troubles to dust like wheat beneath a millstone.'"

"'Should you refuse to allow the son of Khvarazmsha to come, you will invite the ire of my father. The two of you will be set against one another. In time you may find cause to fight, each striving for what he believes to be best for our Kingdom. Your quarrel will make a wasteland of India, and the country will be destroyed. Our enemies will overcome us, and we will be lost to one another.'"

"'Yet, if you allow this trespasser in and we are married, you and I will be forever separated. The joy and gaiety we dressed one another with will be turned to robes of mourning. Meanwhile, those around us will be joyous, celebrating what they believe to be my wish. Our suffering will multiply a hundredfold at the sight of their happiness. I would die, for I would never have it said Persians hold sway in my court.'"

"At the thought of my love married to another, my hand found its way to my sword, and I spoke out. 'God before me, I will not let this wedding come to pass! When these men come here, I will ride out to assess their quality. Then I will show them our true strength and come down on them like a storm. I will ruin every man and animal they bring here, leaving their corpses on the roadside.'"

"Nestan stilled my hand, speaking wisdom in the face of my wrath. 'No, you must not do this. A woman should behave in the manner of her sex, and I will not accept wanton bloodshed. You would make a wall of me, dividing what you seek to protect and hurting us both in the process. Let them enter but do not meet them. Instead, make your way to the son of Khvarazmsha, and kill him. Do not disturb his armies or the men of his guard, for he alone bears this sin.'"

"'This will bring true justice to us, which makes the driest of trees turn green again. You, who are my lion and the most excellent of all heroes, must eliminate the trespasser with stealth. But remember, his men did no harm to you. Do not slaughter them like cattle, or there will be too much innocent blood on your hands. Only one among them has trespassed towards me. Punish him and no other.'"

"'When he is laid low by your hand, tell my father. Make him know the heritage of your country is yours alone, and you will not allow one coin from our Kingdom to be fed to the Persians. If he does not listen and let you rule in peace, tell him you will make a wilderness of the city.'"

"'However, do not say you want my love. Keep your desire for me a secret. This will make the righteousness of your actions greater. The King will become desperate and beg you to act in the interests of India. I will agree to be your wife, and we will marry. When this happens, we will rule together as it should be. This will be the best outcome for us.'"

"The wisdom of this woman I so loved never ceased to amaze me. She had found the way to what we desired, at no more than the cost of a single life. I would only slay he who dared trespass upon what was mine, and in doing so, keep our country intact. Her counsel pleased me, and I rose to leave, so I might prepare."

"She begged me to stay longer. Though I burned to embrace her, I did not let myself take the liberty. Instead, I spent a little more time there before bidding her goodnight. As was our custom, Asmath led me out. But my grief increased a thousandfold as I rode away. Our parting reduced the fire of my joy to no more than a flickering candle."

"I left to prepare for a task I must complete out of necessity rather than want. While honor could be found in protecting the sovereignty of my Kingdom, there was little glory in slaying an unarmed Prince as he slept. Yet my duty was to India and Nestan, and so I went back to the fortress I lived in. When I arrived, I walked towards my rooms with slow and leaden steps. Each foot wishing more than the one before to go in the other direction so I could be next to the sun of my heart."

CHAPTER 41

PATIENCE AND COWARDICE

"In the morning, I woke to the sound of a man shouting through the streets, announcing the bridegroom's arrival. This idiot did not know what fate awaited the foolish Prince for his trespasses. Instead, he went on gleefully bellowing his bit of news to all who would listen. Though he irritated me, duty required my presence at the palace, so I mounted and rode to meet the King."

"When I came to Pharsidan, he embraced me. This man was a father to me, the same as Sheridan, and I loved him deeply. It pained me to know what grief I would soon visit on him, but I could not allow India to fall beneath the boot of Persia."

"He appeared pleased with himself as he greeted me. 'Come and celebrate with me, my son. This is a day of great joy, for your sister Nestan is to be wed. Help me and send a man to bring all the treasures from vaults. We will shower the groom and his party with gifts. To do less would be foolish, for when he is King, the entire country will belong to him anyway.'"

"There are times in every man's life when he must bite his tongue, but those words caused me to chew mine to ribbons with restraint. My tongue hung in my mouth like a tattered flag, torn to pieces by the treachery duty forced me to utter. As requested, I ordered the men of our castle to distribute the bounty of my Kingdom to these foreign trespassers. I had no choice but to watch servants spill the blood of my country to appease the loathsome formalities of court."

"And come they did, for soon the fields outside around us overflowed with more foreigners than we were able to contain. As my city and heart were invaded, my foster father spoke again. 'Instruct your men to prepare a place for the bridegroom to rest. You will meet him in the palace tomorrow. For now, your Knights and soldiers are sufficient to do him homage.'"

"I commanded tents of rich red satin to be raised in the square and filled with all manner of comforts. Hot baths were prepared, and an endless stream of fruits and delicacies were delivered to satisfy the Prince and his retinue. When the man arrived, I observed him as he rode in. From a distance, one might mistake their arrival for the celebration of Easter Eve, but I knew better. The son of Khvarazmsha came with a host of courtiers and was flanked by soldiers from many different regions."

"They formed disciplined ranks to either side of the streets as he made his way to the resting place we prepared, but the lie unfolding before me was more than I could bear. I understood patience would serve me best but craved a quick end to this affront. Before long, he settled into his pavilion, ringed with soldiers."

"The weight of duty bore down on me, and I grew weary of delaying my hand. I mounted my horse and left the palace, wishing to sleep. However, as I turned towards my home, a man caught my attention with a letter."

"Though tired, I saw it was from Nestan and was pleased to receive news from my love. She ordered me to come immediately, and I quickly rode to the walled garden around her tower. When I arrived, I found Asmath in a heap, weeping uncontrollably."

"I helped her stand, asking why she cried so, and she answered between sobs. 'How can I avoid tears when I am forever engaged in your defense? I unceasingly justify you and your actions to her, yet she does not listen. Through no choice of mine, I am your advocate, for I would not see either of you separated from the other.'"

"Then she opened the gilded curtains, still weeping, and I followed her in. Nestan stood there, shining with such intensity I felt the entirety of our Kingdom might be set aflame from her eyes alone. I readied myself to greet her, but before I could speak, her tongue struck like the blade of an assassin. 'You deceived me again with your falsehoods! Look at you, standing here like a coward when the day of battle is upon us. Does your heart lack the strength to do what we agreed or are you not the man you pretend to be?!'"

CHAPTER 42

THE SLEEPING PRINCE

"Until this moment, there had never been anger in my heart towards Nestan. Yet, the audacity of her accusations pierced my soul, and my spirit burst into flame. I turned and walked away from her without a word. When the curtain fell between us and I was a few steps away, I shouted back over my shoulder to her, 'Do not think me so cowardly as to need a woman to urge me into a fight! Now you will see the truth of my promise, though I did not desire it to be public.'"

"I left in a blind rage, intent on nothing but slaughter. When I returned to my castle, I summoned a hundred of my best Knights, the same who remained living from those who had stood beside me against Ramaz and his treachery. When they arrived, I made myself clear."

"'It poisons me to sit idle while the Kingship is passed to a Persian. I am the last Prince of India. By right, no one should rule but me. If you would bow your knee to the son of Khvarazmsha, you deserve the yoke he will place about your neck. But if you are true to our Kingdom, come with me. I go now to slay him and end this.'"

"My men all felt like me and agreed to my course. None wanted their homeland parceled off to invaders. Together, we mounted and rode to the palace. Once there, we slipped from our horses and stealthily made our way through the city. No one was aware of us as we approached the sleeping Prince."

"I crept up to his tent and sliced through the back edge with my knife. Slipping in, I observed him lying in bed, drunk and snoring. His debauchery disgusted me, and I grabbed him by the legs, dashing his head against the center support pole so hard I cracked it, striking him dead. As promised, I shed no blood in the deed, though other men would bleed soon enough."

"The noise of his head splitting woke the courtiers sleeping by the entrance. They cried in terror when they realized what I did to their Lord. This alerted his guards, and they stormed in, but I was already gone back the way I came. Almost instantly, an alarm went up amongst his soldiers."

"They pursued my Knights and me, but we knew the land better. Those who came close to us were slain. We did not lose a single man, protected by our armor and skill. Soon we reached the walls of my fortress. Once within, we could not be touched, for my castle was impregnable. I was Amirbar."

"I sent messengers to notify the soldiers of India of what I had done, requesting all loyal men to join me on the plains around my home. We would not tolerate insolence from our enemy. Their leader was dead, and I would rule. Still, Persians tried to make their way to us throughout the night. We cut them all down, save those few who recognized me and retreated, keeping their heads intact."

"I arose at daybreak after a brief rest and put on my armor. When I went to inspect my troops, I found three lords waiting for me. They carried a letter from Pharsidan. 'Tariel, I raised you as my own. If you wanted to marry my daughter, why didn't you tell me? Why did you repay me by turning my joy into grief?'"

"'You spilled the innocent blood of Khvarazmsha's son on the steps of our house. How will I reconcile his death at your hands without war? What will happen to the Kingdom? Worse, what will become of you? You brought a thing on yourself which will cause us to be separated. My life will be unbearable, for you will not sit beside me in my later years.'"

"Seeing my foster father so wounded by my actions tore my heart to shreds, but I wrote my response, answering him as I had agreed with Nestan. 'I am stronger than steel. Do not worry about my safety. The flames of fire and death will not destroy me, but as you know better than me, a King must dispense justice. I swear by your virtue I did not do this to seek flattery. This man was a trespasser and received what he deserved.'"

"'It is unjust God gave you no son, but I am far from desiring your daughter. While the heritage of our Kingdom remains with you, I must ask, where are the other heirs? Of the seven thrones and palaces, I am the only one remaining. By right, the Lordship is mine.'"

"'If you give my rule to Khvarazmsha, what is left to me? How can another King be seated in India while I still wear my sword? This is my country, and I will destroy any man who contests my right to the throne. May God strike me down if I call on the aid of foreigners to claim my birthright!'"

CHAPTER 43

BEHIND THE THRONE

"With my letter composed, I sent it back to Pharsidan in the hands of the three Lords. I did not fear what would come, for I was in the right. More, Nestan supported me. With her by my side, there was nothing I could not accomplish. Yet, I still had no news from her. This worried me, adding fuel to the fires in my soul. I began to pace, and after a time, I went to walk the walls of my fortress. Looking over the plains, I learned a dreadful thing.'"

"Two disheveled people approached. One clearly a servant of the other, but both bloodied and weary from whatever ordeal they endured. Soon I recognized one as Asmath. Her head was not covered, and she stumbled as she walked. I quickly came down to the gates, running across the plain to meet her and shouting as I approached. 'What happened?'"

"Yet she did not answer. When I came closer, I understood how damaged she was. Her clothes were filthy, and blood matted her once fine hair. It ran down her face, staining the breast of her robes a bright red. She could not stand alone and leaned on the man for support. As I reached her side, she collapsed in a faint."

"I picked her up and carried her back. When I put her down, I wiped her face, and she woke. For a moment, she looked at me in a daze, as if unaware of who I was, before weeping pitifully. I tried calming her with reassurances as to her safety within my castle, but nothing consoled her. After a long time, she spoke one sentence before falling into tears once more. 'The Heavens have rained wrath down on us for what we did.'"

"Despite my efforts, she said no more. Clearly, grief consumed her. I grew mad to learn about Nestan, or why Asmath and her servant were so bloody and beaten. Yet, as I knew nothing, I could not take action or ease her worry."

"Finally, the storm of her sorrow abated enough for her to speak. 'I will tell you of events, but you must swear to show mercy when I finish speaking. Fulfill your duty and separate me from this life I now hate. I beg of you, have pity. Spare me passing another day in this bitter world.'"

"'When you struck down the son of Khvarazmsha, the alarm they raised alerted Pharsidan and the palace guard. He leaped up, stricken by news of the murder, and searched everywhere for you. When no one was able to find you, he realized it was you who felled the Prince. His anger was boundless, leaving him shouting at everyone, but he was not angry with you. Instead, he directed his fury at his sister.'"

"'Unbeknownst to any of us, he knew you loved his daughter, and she you. When you returned from your victory over Ramaz, he noticed the two of you looking at one another. It gave him joy, but he feared you would keep your feelings secret to avoid offending him.'"

"'He turned to Davar for advice, and she counseled him to arrange marriage to a foreigner. This was done so you would speak up and insist on your right to the Lordship. But the King always wanted you marry his daughter. If you spoke for her, he would send the trespasser home to his father and give her hand to you.'"

"'Yet, when you killed the man, Pharsidan realized he had been tricked by his sister's schemes, for she was wise in the deceitful ways of a Kadj. He understood her plans then, as it was her counsel which led you to wrath. He swore by his head if he suffered her to live, he would renounce God. By his order, she and her lovers were to be publicly executed as punishment for their meddling.'"

"'Somehow, by her sorcery or the whispers of a traitor to

India, she learned of his intent. Knowing this, she came to our garden with sweet words. None stopped her or gave pause, as she was Nestan's teacher. She easily made her way into the tower, where I sat with your sun.'"

"'Nestan wore the veil and cloak you gave her, radiant and lovely. Yet Davar stormed in like a drunken sailor, breaking the peace of our rest. She surprised and shocked us both with foul words no one spoke in our presence before that day. The things she said would make a soldier blush, and they wilted your rose.'"

"'She called Nestan a whore, saying she was a wanton and loose woman who made herself available to any man passing by. Davar told us she knew her brother would execute her, and said before her life ended, she would leave no cause for rejoicing between you and your moon. With a mad grin, she beat the pale face of your angel, dragging her by the hair and bruising her with fists and insults.'"

"'Apparently, when you killed the son of Khvarazmsha, it ruined whatever evil Davar planned. Yet, she would not be content in fleeing with her life. She refused to die in vain for the trouble her actions caused. Calling on God as her witness, she cursed Nestan to never lay eyes on you again, or you upon her so long as either of you lived.'"

"'Torn and bleeding, your love crumpled on hearing those words. She wept ceaselessly, but no one could stop Davar. Two brutish Kadj men had come in with her, black as pitch and with shining golden teeth. They slaughtered the guards outside our garden and brought a large bound chest with them. They opened it and shoved Nestan inside. She shouted and cried for our help, but they struck us down when we tried to stop them. Of us all, only we two survived.'"

"'I woke in a pool of blood from my broken head and the servants who had been slain, unable to rise or move more than my eyes. Yet, I heard the witch as she uttered the last of her curse, ordering those brutes to take their prize into the great seas. Their instructions were to avoid the frozen waters to the south, and not to leave her in sweet water. Instead, they should dump her on the shores of the farthest sea, where none would ever find her.'"

"'Those evil men laughed with joy, insulting Nestan as they lifted the chest between them. They made their way down the road towards the seaport until her screams and cries faded into the distance. When they had gone, Davar sat down, thinking no one saw her.'"

"'She asked God who among all men would not stone her to death for the evil of her actions. Laughing, she looked to the Heavens, saying she was weary of living anyway, and would end her own life before Pharsidan had the opportunity. Still cackling in her madness, she drew a dagger from her robes and cut her throat, falling into a stream of her own blood.'"

"'I saw everything but was powerless to stop it. How I wished to die rather than witness this! I came to you, who alone has the strength to save her. But now I beg you, release me from this unbearable life I now endure. Free me from this hollow and empty husk!'"

"When she finished speaking, Asmath threw herself to the ground in front of me. Tears fell from her eyes, burning drops of misery spilled from an ocean of guilt. I searched my soul and found words to comfort her and soothe the wounds on her heart. Kneeling beside her, with my hand on her head, I said, 'Sister mine, why would I kill you? There is no wrong with anything you did. It is good you came. Without you, all would be lost.'"

"'Now I am aware of what mischief Davar engineered, I can begin to look for our rose. My debt to your strength and service is immeasurable. I swear I will search for Nestan her over the whole of the earth. Wherever rocks and water are found or any other place I may roam, you and I will find her together. She is not lost to us. Do not despair.'"

"Though I spoke words of encouragement, my heart was petrified. A forest of stone grew within me, and I became mad, trembling uncontrollably. Yet, I could not allow my steps to falter. One day was already gone since they stole my sun. Now an endless sea awaited, and I had no shortage of preparations to make."

CHAPTER 44

INTO THE SILENT SEA

"The Prince lay dead, slain by my hand. There was no doubt his father would answer with war. If I stayed to defend India, Nestan would be lost forever. Yet, if I left to find her, I would not be able to protect my country. Though perhaps a difficult choice to some, there was no question in my heart of what I would do. Life meant nothing to me without her. I would search over the whole earth if necessary."

"With my decision made, I called the master of my guard, and he summoned my Knights. I selected the same hundred from their number as who had come with me to slay the Prince, and another sixty soldiers to manage our supplies and gear. The rest of my armies stayed behind to fortify the castles and secure the palace when the Persians attacked, as they surely would. Asmath and her servant also accompanied us."

"Soon, we passed through the gates of my fortress in a tight battle formation, the thunder of our march echoing across the plains. Though groups of armed men waited for us, they were unable to match us. We scattered them like chaff to the winds."

"When we came to the city, it was in complete disarray. Soldiers of the King mixed with mine, and others still from the son of Khvarazmsha. They fought small battles in the streets, which we simply rode through. None gave any significant challenge to us, and we made it to the port without delay."

"Once there, my men scoured the docks for news of the two Kadj men or my beloved. But unfortunately, we learned nothing, so I hailed the Captain of an Indian warship. He recognized me as Amirbar and asked how he might serve us. When I told him of Nestan's kidnapping, he invited us to board at once."

"His ship was well stocked. More, we carried our own supplies and chests of gold to restock ourselves if the search took us to distant ports. If I knew then what I know now, perhaps I would have set us on a different course."

"Once we boarded, his oarsmen rowed us out of the harbor. When we reached the open sea, they raised sails and we spent all day challenging everyone we passed. We searched every vessel, large or small. Yet for all our efforts, we found no sign of Nestan, and none who knew of the men we sought."

"Weeks went by like this, but no other ship or crew had any information. I grew desperate with worry to find her. My blood boiled with wrath. But for all my strength and fury, I could direct my anger nowhere other than at myself."

"At each port, I sent small parties of men looking for her. They were instructed to return with news the next morning, or if they found nothing, depart for India to inform Pharsidan our search continued. Meanwhile, the rest of us made our way across what seemed to be a silent sea."

"Occasionally, we met other merchant ships, but none ever carried word of what we hoped for. Other times pirates attacked or refused to stop, forcing us to board them. Each time I looked for news but was always disappointed. No one could tell us anything."

"One year passed like this, but it felt like two for me. The hull and rigging of our ship were battered and beaten from the long voyage, and only two of my Knights remained with us. One who studied languages and history while the other was learned in surgery and medicines. Besides these two, only Asmath was by my side."

"The loss of those who accompanied me to this misfortune pained my heart. Some had perished in battles, while others were scattered by duty or need. The manner of their passing did not matter to my conscience. Each man gone marked another wound added to the gaping hole in me."

"I grew mad for want of my nightingale. Sorrow became a joy to me and slowly gnawed at my sanity. Resigned to Fate, I decided whatever was willed upon me would be. I could not deny Heaven any more than I might stop the sun from rising. But though my misery was great, I did not believe God would abandon a man so forsaken by fortune."

"This kept an ember of hope alive in my heart, enabling me to continue searching for Nestan."

CHAPTER 45

A MAN AND HIS HORSE

"One evening, we sailed to a cove on the shores of a far land. A city could be seen in the distance, but I did not desire meeting or conversing with men yet. The brands of betrayal and misery still scarred my heart. I had no interest in speaking to another, let alone sharing the tale of my woe. However, I was weary of seeing water and had set my mind to abandon the ship. I would send the captain home, though he bore no good news for Pharsidan."

"I took a longboat and rowed towards the beach, with only Asmath and my two remaining Knights. We came to shore near a grove of tall trees, and I left the boat first, leaping to the land. At first, the ground was a strange thing to me. My body no longer moved to the rhythm of the sea or shifted with every swell and wave, and the earth beneath my feet gave me hope, weary though I was."

"We would need supplies to continue our search across the lands, but before I dared speak to anyone, I needed to rest and compose myself. So, while the others made camp and prepared food, I found a comfortable place under the trees, soon falling into a deep and dreamless sleep."

"I woke not long after and was reminded again of the pain of my loss. Though the smell of bread baking over our fire stirred my hunger, the soot of my scorched heart blacked out any joy or peace I might have felt. In a year of searching, I learned nothing. It seemed one sorrow piled on top of the other."

"Each day I felt my life slipping away like the lives of my men, as though I held fists full of sand. I knew nothing of India or what came of my actions against Khvarazmsha, but I did not care. My heart and soul were focused only on finding news of my beloved, though I had thus far failed to learn even gossip of her whereabouts."

"Though I did not want to rise, duty beckoned. Without me, no hope remained of rescuing Nestan, yet standing felt like an impossible task. I would have preferred the world to reach up and envelop me so I could fade back into the dirt from whence I had been born."

"Lost to my misery, I did not see or hear the stranger galloping toward us until his cry caught my attention. I looked up at the sound and saw a young Knight approaching. The magnificent black steed he rode set an unbelievable pace down the shore, like a Pegasus with midnight wings. As for the man, he wore long mustaches and was holding a broken sword. Arrows stuck out from his sides, and blood flowed from his many wounds. He cursed those who must have attacked him, though none appeared to be in pursuit."

"Jumping up from my resting place, I girded my armor, intent on meeting the man. I ordered one of my Knights to stop him, but whatever my man said did not reach the stranger, for he never slowed or acknowledged them. I ran forward into his path, calling out to him. 'Stay yourself! Tell me what happened, and perhaps I may be of assistance.'"

"Pulling up his horse, the Knight stopped and stared at me. Surprise and admiration etched his face, despite his obvious pain. He looked up then and addressed the Heavens. 'My God, how did you make such a tree as this man who appears from nowhere to grace my sight?'"

"Looking back down, he grimaced at me, barely maintaining his seat, and spoke. 'Though I do not know who you are or where you come from, I am spent. I mistook my enemies for goats, but they proved to be lions. Like traitors, they fell on me as one. Neither my sword nor armor were readied for battle, leaving me woefully unprepared for their attack. Thus, you see me now, wounded of body and spirit, yet still clinging to life. I pray less misfortune will come to me from our meeting.'"

"Of all the people had I met in my journeys, I never saw anyone like the man who sat on the horse before me. Despite swooning from his injuries, he gave grace to God and honored me, though I was a stranger to him. I instantly respected his character."

"I spoke to him as I called my men to attend him. 'Do not fear my intent, fair Knight. I am no enemy to you. Though it is not valorous to withdraw from combat when wounded, treachery is another matter. Let us help you dismount. We will tend your wounds and ailments.'"

"As I helped him off his horse and led him to our camp, I noticed what a lion the man was. When my surgeon removed the arrows and stitched his many sword cuts, he didn't once cry out. In truth, I could not believe he was still standing, let alone had the strength to converse."

"After we bound his wounds, the five of us rested. We shared our camp and broke bread together. As he spoke, his openness surprised me, for age and experience often breed distrust among strangers. Yet, he was a youth. Perhaps he did not know better, or there was some secret to him I had not discovered. Curious to learn more, I asked who he was and how he came to be wounded so grievously."

CHAPTER 46

BROTHERS AND BETRAYAL

"Looking up at the heavens, the Knight gave a long sigh, deep in thought. His mustaches drooped down the sides of his mouth, and he put his hand to them before at last speaking. 'I do not know who you are. Nor who I can compare you to. When I look at you, there is a mystery before me.'"

"'Here sits a man once full, who is now consumed by something. Though you appear formed of rose and jet, you are sallower than amber. I wonder why God put out the candle he lit himself when creating you. Still, I will share my story with you stranger, as you have shared your hospitality with me.'"

"'I am Nuridon Phridon. In the distance is my city, Mulghazanzar. It is my home, and I am King. These lands we sit in are the boundary of my Kingdom. Though my domain is small, every part is of the highest quality. You will find no slums or poor quarters in or out of our walls.'"

"'My people are artisans and scholars, and warriors as well. Our battles are those of science and of the mind. We do not seek conquest of land but rather of self. Because of this, we do not gather lands and people, as others who hold the Lordship are wont to do. Therein lies the tale of my tragedy.'"

"'My grandfather shared his Kingdom between my father and his brother. Yet, they were not men of the same character. My father was a scholar and a warrior like his father before him and like me. Whereas my uncle only cared about conquering others and acquiring wealth. Though different, they loved one another as brothers, or so I thought until today.'"

"'Not far from here rests an island in the sea, which is part of the territory my father was given dominion over. Though it is home to my uncle's fortress, one side is mine by right and remains largely uninhabited. The hunting is excellent there, and my father shared it as a place of sport. Unfortunately, today I learned the legacy of our family has been betrayed by my cousins, for they tried to bring about my ruin.'"

"'Early this morning, I came near where we sit now. I wanted to be alone and left my troops home so I could roam the shores with only a few falconers and beaters. We hoped to find sport, but the tall trees in this place blocked our falcons from pursuing game. In time I decided to visit the island areas my father gave me.'"

"'We rowed a longboat across the sea to the mouth of a small creek. Though I was surprised at how many people I saw, I did not fear those of my own blood. I was his brother's son, and we had no reason to argue.'"

"'I enjoyed myself, shouting as we pursued our prey. The falcons brought down almost everything we chased up, and I shot what was left with my bow. Taking this time alone had filled me with joy, and I thought the day was wonderful. Yet the family of my uncle did not share my happiness. They felt I had scorned them because I sought my own space rather than seeking them out for conversation.'"

"'While I hunted, they secretly surrounded me with soldiers, going so far as to block the way back to my ship. Their treachery might have succeeded, but I heard them in the bush and noticed the flash of their blades. When I realized there were men hiding in the bushes, we quickly retreated, but too many of them attacked us. I shouted out, hoping to avert an accident, for I assumed they had mistaken us for invaders. But then I saw my cousin at their head.'"

"'He lowered his arm and pointed at me, ordering his men towards where I stood. It was then I understood his intent. They knew I left my Knights at home and had decided to murder me in secret. His troops rushed us, cutting down the first of us as they sought to overcome me.'"

"'Men leaped from hiding, swords flashing and bows singing as they tried to kill me. My remaining falconers and I raced towards the shore, breaking through their ranks. We shouted to the boatman but could not reach him.'"

"'They slaughtered everyone with me, but I would not let them take my head so easily. I fought until my blade broke and I was forced to retreat before being overwhelmed. Yet still, they followed, firing one volley after another or arrows at me. More men came from behind, and they also chased me, but I pulled ahead of them.'"

"'Not one man who came with me survived the betrayal of my uncle and his sons, but they were could not overpower me with numbers. Seeking freedom from their treachery, I urged my horse over their men and into the water. I managed to swim far enough away that they left me to a watery grave, but the sea did not take me. She spit me back on the beach, and I did not die.'"

"'Now, I pray to Heaven for the strength to seek justice against them in my father's name. My honor will not allow me to let the lives of those who came with me go unavenged. At this moment, I wish nothing more than to make them lament their existence. I hope to bring the wrath of God down upon their heads and call the crows to make a banquet of their corpses.'"

"When Phridon finished his story, I fully understood the manner of his character and gave my heart to the youth. He was honorable and proud, reminding me of myself in no small way. Yet I also found in his cause a balm to soothe the wounds which seared me, and I offered to help him."

"'My friend, it is unwise to rush back into a den of vipers. Heal yourself first, and I will accompany you to their ruin. They will not stand against the two of us. We will bring doom upon those who betrayed the honor and dignity of their own blood. This I swear to you.'"

"'For me, I will tell you the full measure of my tragedy in time. No doubt you are desperate to learn my tale, but we must first tend to your needs. We will help you safely back to your city and the people of Mulghazanzar. To do less would be unbecoming, for we are both Knights and Lords in our own rights. Now, let us rest and ready ourselves for tomorrow.'"

"When I finished speaking, Phridon looked at me with a mix of bewilderment and joy before answering. 'Who are you to come from nowhere and so willingly offer yourself to the service of my cause? If my uncle and his son were a tenth the man you are, I would have no reason for grief. I will remain indebted to your aid until the day of my death and forever be a friend devoted to you.'"

CHAPTER 47

THE CITY OF MULGHAZANZAR

"We spent the night on the shores, telling tales of our cities and ourselves. To my surprise, Asmath smiled more than once at the stories Phridon told. For me, I forgot the woe brooding over my heart and looked at the stars for the first time in a year. Rather than the weight of Heaven bearing down on me, the soft lights kindled a glimmer of hope in my soul."

"In the morning, we left our camp and made our way to Mulghazanzar. It was small, as the Knight said. But true to his word, it was the fairest place I had seen. A wall of towering white stone blocks ringed the city, marvelous to behold. Defenses more advanced than anything I knew from my years of war lined the battlements."

"The most impressive thing remained unseen until we entered. There, to my amazement, everything appeared shaped by the hands of master craftsmen. Not a single building or cobblestone lay in disrepair, and there was no poor quarter. No beggars or pickpockets came seeking coins, and merchants carried the finest wares. It was truly a city of the wise, and my pleasure to set foot within those walls."

"As we entered, soldiers appeared by the hundreds. Many embraced him, kissing the hilt and broken blade of his sword, while others took dirt from the earth and covered themselves in shame. I was confused by their behavior, until learning his people believed him lost. The search party they sent feared the worst when they found blood on the island. Soon after, they asked his uncle's son for news. He told them pirates had set upon Phridon, slaying him and his hunters."

"When the soldiers and citizens learned the truth, the entire city stood ready to seek justice. They compared him to the sun and praised his worth over the unrefined children of his uncle. One after another, people came to welcome their King home, each of them wearing fine clothes. In all my travels I met no better dressed or educated men and women. Nor did I see any so devoted to their Lord."

"Yet he was far from healed, and still bore many wounds. Healers and Wisemen came as we helped him from his horse. Though he pushed them away, they would not be denied. Eventually he relented, allowing them to fret over his injuries. They brought salves and medicines I had never seen, and their methods surprised and intrigued my surgeon. So, I gave him leave to go with them, for the exchange of new ideas always benefits the wise."

"For our part, we were given apartments in the palace while our new friend was restored to health. My two men busied themselves over the weeks with sharing knowledge and learning from those of the city while Asmath and I rested. She and I shared our griefs and hopes with one another, each urging the other to carry on."

"Though I did not wish to share my tale with anyone, she insisted I had no choice. She reminded me I would be forever shamed if I refused and broke my word, for I promised to tell my story once we overcame Phridon's adversaries. I did not want to, but as is so often the case, her wisdom ruled over my judgment."

"Some weeks later, Phridon came out from the hospitals. I could not believe how fast he recovered. He was transformed into a whole man again, and worthy of praise to God above. He stood like a lion carved of ivory and ebony. His eyes glowed a soft yet piercing blue without depth or measure, reminding me of morning skies when I was a child, while the white of his face shone like a moon. The black of his mustaches appeared woven from wisps of night, and his voice held the timbre of deep harp strings. Though we broke bread before, it seemed I looked on a different man now."

"In celebration of his recovery, we feasted. The entirety of his Kingdom joined us, each bringing new and wonderful delicacies with them. Everyone took turns singing and playing various instruments, but none celebrated more than he. We gave thanks to Heaven for our newfound friendship, as made promises and vows of brotherhood to one another."

"When the revelry of our evening ended, we stayed late into the night pouring over maps and discussing how best to attack the fortress of his uncle. Over the next few days our plan was decided, and we readied his armies. We would bring ruin on his betrayers."

"He split his soldiers into groups, with the bulk of his men assigned to assault the island. A smaller body would remain behind to protect the city in the event of a counterattack. I accompanied the main group of his army, and we boarded our warships, one man to an oar. To our good fortune, the winds blew in our favor."

"Each ship was overflowing with hosts of his best soldiers. Had I filled them with my own Knights, I would have only equaled the might arrayed before me. If our enemy knew what awaited their folly, they would have prayed to God for aid."

"Phridon was a lion among those gathered, and I did not doubt of the punishment his adversaries would soon face. He walked on the deck of the lead ship, and I rode in another next to his. We smiled and saluted one another, ready for war as we sailed towards the battle. Yet before we made land, the ships of his treacherous uncle came upon us.

CHAPTER 48

THE WAR OF THE ISLAND

"It seemed his uncle had secretly planned an assault on Mulghazanzar after believing him dead, so they were surprised to see our warships already prepared and on the sea. Yet, when we saw our enemy approaching, we understood their plans and realized just how treacherous they truly were. A fierce cry went up from our men at that moment."

"The wind was behind us, and lent aid to our sails as the drums beat faster and our ships reached ramming speed. Phridon crashed into their first vessel, spectacularly sinking it with a single hit. I counted perhaps eight more of their boats remaining, but in the heat of battle, I cannot swear if there were more or less."

"It did not matter how many they had though, for we came prepared. The fools who challenged us would soon meet watery graves. I shouted encouragement as my crew hit the side of an enemy vessel. Desperate to wet my blade with the blood of our enemies, I leaped from my place, landing on the deck of our foe. I struck like a whirlwind of steel. My strikes leaving men headless or clutching at the last of their life as it bled from the wounds I gifted them with."

"Then we flew from one ship to the next, our wrath more certain than the doom I had once visited on Ramaz and his armies. One after another, their soldiers fell to our onslaught until those remaining took small boats and rowed for shore as if Poseidon himself pursued them."

"Unwilling to let them all escape, I forced my heel on one of the boats they fled in, spilling the men into the water where the weight of their armor pulled them into the grasp of the deep. All about us, those who wished to harm us wailed like children, weeping and crying at the folly of their actions. Yet we would not be stopped."

"We slaughtered every man we encountered. Those who escaped the force of our initial assault made their way to the harbor, but their respite was short lived. Before long, we landed our own ships. Our men disembarked, some few were struck by arrows while others made their way into the bushes and cut down the archers."

"Where before men had fought against me and the sea for their lives, now Phridon and I battered them between us like small ships caught between waves and a cliff. We stood beside one another as lions guarding the temple of honor. Our faces shone down on our enemies, burning them like twin suns. Soon we came upon his treacherous cousins."

"They sought to overcome him together, but he beat them to the ground with the ferocity of his attacks. Once they fell, he did not kill them. Instead, he cut their sword hands off and left them wailing in misery as their blood darkened the sand. Those who witnessed the fate of their Lords broke ranks and ran, fleeing towards the far side of the island."

"Our Knights let out a cheer, and we pursued the cowards as they fled, picking off traitors as we went. A handful met us in valorous combat, but most we butchered like the filth they were. Those few who reached to the safety of their city enjoyed little time for celebration."

"Our engineers cracked open their fortifications like an oyster, and we tore down their gates and battlements in our wrath. We broke the legs of those who stood against us with stones from the walls and flayed the skin from others. When we finished, not a man from our enemy remained uninjured."

"With victory in our hands, Phridon rallied his men. They searched for survivors, leaving no one alive who fought us. The betrayers who submitted were humiliated and marched to the center of town. Meanwhile, he and I entered the castle to seize the treasury. When we opened the vaults, I could not believe the riches they held."

"Clearly, his uncle had been pillaging passing ships, perhaps sharing information on merchant vessels and then attacking the pirates who raided them. It seemed betrayal was all they knew, for no other means would have allowed them to acquire such wealth. Once we secured the treasuries, we returned to the square."

"Turning to the people, he informed them of his Lordship. Those who wished to leave were given gold in exchange for their holds and escorted to the next Kingdom. Whoever chose to remain swore their allegiance to Phridon. Then, in front of those who stayed, he took his two traitorous cousins into the fields and spilled what remained of their blood into the dirt, returning them to the earth whose kinship they had betrayed."

"He left their bodies in the field for the crows to feast on and a garrison of a hundred good men to defend the city. The rest of our soldiers loaded the bulk of the treasures onto our ships, and we made ready for our return. Then, he sent messengers back to Mulghazanzar requesting artisans and supplies. They would rebuild the town and improve the lives of those living there. When I asked why he did this, he shared the wisdom of his father with me."

"Phridon told me it takes no more than three generations for intelligence to slip into ignorance. Yet, a man can grow his people into something better in one generation, teaching them to work for the common good. Citizens, he said, are like the crops they tend. When properly cared for, their wisdom ripens as they age. No different than grapes from a vine, it is the hand of the vintner which determines the quality of wine produced."

"As he spoke, I learned his grandfather had applied the same philosophies to the people of Mulghazanzar, which was why the Knight viewed it as his duty to improve this city. He would teach the people what they were capable of, rather than focusing on their past failures. The idea was novel to me, and a form of governing unlike any I knew of."

"Of course, Phridon was not like anyone I had met before then or since. I witnessed this anew when we returned to his city. All throughout the streets, his people celebrated. Sellers gave their wares freely. Jugglers and performers danced and threw fire in the air, while poets recited newly composed tales praising their King. Unlike other rulers, he did not need to call for celebrations. The people recognized and valued him for who he was, and not what he ordered from them."

"Soldiers paraded us around on their shoulders as if we were sergeants instead of Lords. They proclaimed his Lordship and further sang me into their songs as a King from afar. Then, as his men gave their allegiance to him forever, he swore his own oath to me as a brother and an equal."

"A contagious joy surrounded me, but my smile did not reach its fullest. My heart was a graveyard of the hopes and dreams Nestan and I once shared. Inside, I was filled with gloom, but none among the guests or our new friends were aware of my story. It was not a thing lightly spoken of."

CHAPTER 49

MOON OVER THE SEA

"In the morning, I came down to the city and found townsfolk cleaning the streets from the celebration the night before. I had never seen those who owned residences tending common areas. That was always a task left to servants and slaves. When I asked a young couple what they were doing, they stared at me in confusion before answering. 'This is our city, so we clean. Are things not the same in your Kingdom?' But what might I say to them? I came from far lands, different than here and perhaps not for the better in some ways."

"The next weeks passed similarly. I constantly learned new things about the customs of these people. While it was interesting and educational, none of it truly mattered to me one way or the other. Like a man in a cave, I no longer counted the days or marked their events. Without Nestan, the passage of time meant nothing."

"I existed to no end, and my heart withered. Yet I did not possess the liberty to die. So instead, I clung to a life none would envy. Though I smiled and laughed with others when they celebrated, in truth, I had no idea where to point my compass. Phridon sensed this and made himself my constant companion. We often hunted together in the farthest corners of his Kingdom, which is perhaps what saved me."

"On one such day, we climbed high up onto a cape jutting out over the water. The view was spectacular, and I recognized the island his deceitful cousins met their end on. Yet farther beyond, one could watch distant ships pass over the curve of the world. This place held rare beauty, and I said as much to my friend."

"He turned to me when I told him this and shared a story with me. 'From here, I once witnessed a thing like nothing else before or since. Some might say it was a mirage, but my eyes did not deceive me, as you will learn.'"

"'On the day I speak of, I came to hunt. My faithful steed sat beneath me as I tracked the flight of my hawks while they brought birds to the ground. The sport pleased me, and after a time, I came where we sit now. I gazed over the vast expanse of sea before me and noticed the smallest of vessels on the horizon. It appeared as no more than a speck of dust on the ocean. Yet, whatever this thing was, light shone from it like the setting sun.'"

"'I watched as the object moved closer, amazed by its speed. Perhaps the hand of God carried it, for no ship I know of can travel so swiftly across the sea. While marvelous to behold, I wondered who piloted the craft and what they might want. As they neared, I waited to see what they would do.'"

"'In time they came closer to the shore, and I made out a small and ornate golden boat. The finest silks covered all sides, so none might easily see what lay within. Yet as the wind blew, I caught a glimpse inside and laid eyes on the moon herself. I swear to you now, she commands my heart to this day. Had I the means, I would give her the Seventh Heaven as a home.'"

"'When they landed on the beach, the maiden came to the edge of the boat, accompanied by two large men with skin black as pitch. They helped her disembark, and she wandered between them and the trees. Her eyes flashed like caged lightning, and she wore her hair down. Thick tresses clung to her like well-aged vines. If I possessed words to describe her honestly, the sun would cease to shine.'"

"'Seeing her filled me with joy, and I desired nothing more than to make myself known to them. I hastily rode down the side of this cliff. You have seen how my horse is like a falcon on the land and a fish on the water. He can vanish from the field or likewise approach without a whisper. Yet, despite the power of my steed and his manner of crossing all obstacles as if nothing, we never reached them.'"

"'However fast I came, they went faster. In the end, I arrived in an empty camp. Their ship was a distant spot on the horizon, and I had no way to catch them. Before long, they vanished from sight. Other than those moments, I never learned more of them.'"

"I listened, and knew it was Nestan, though he did not realize it. The flames of loss burned my heart with renewed intensity, and I lost my composure. I threw myself to the ground, yelling at the Heavens and shouting in rage and frustration."

"If I died then, it would have been preferable to me. It made me sick to think of my rose subject to a will than her own. Worse, I became unreasonably mad thinking of any man other than me looking on her."

"Phridon witnessed this and tried to console me, though I am sure my behavior confused him. He pitied me as I lay in my misery, soothing and calming me with care and concern. Unfortunately, my grief drowned out all else, and his words were lost to me."

"At one point, he shook my shoulders, shouting at me and begging to know what was wrong. 'I am sorry for whatever I did, but I am here to help. What did I say to ruin you so utterly? Tell me!'"

"He brought me back to reason, and I took deep breaths of the sea air, choking on the sorrow which moments before threatened to engulf me. Then I explained how my sudden woe had nothing to do with his actions. He did nothing wrong but rather a great deed for me."

"I searched so long for news of her. Yet, Phridon had no idea of this, and I bore him no anger. My will was spent. I broke down and shared all my troubles over the last few years. He learned every moment of my story from start to finish, no different from what I tell you now. I told him because he wished to be my brother and comrade in arms. Accepting such an honor from him without also detailing the burden it carried would be an injustice."

"I explained to him how the sun of my heart rose and set on her every movement, sharing the battles I fought to win her love. He listened intently, learning of the intrigue leading to Prince Khvarazmsha's death. I described the two Kadj men who kidnapped Nestan, and he confirmed their descriptions as the men on the boat. Yet telling my tale did not lessen the fires consuming me. I did not know what to do. In the end, my mind became a brand burning me to ash."

"Still upset, my friend tried to console me. 'I am ashamed of my mistake, for I did not know my words would bring you to ruin. You are King of the Indians. A ruler mightier than me by a hundred thousand times. A royal seat and throne are more suited to you than this place, yet here you sit with me.'"

"'Why do you forget this? A man such as you cannot be formed without his heart being pierced by a spear. Though the pain may lacerate you, do not despair. The will of God is beyond either of us to understand. We can only be certain of his mercy, which thunders down from Heaven and changes sorrow to joy as rain turns the fields from brown to green. Those who trust in Him and keep their faith never grieve without cause.'"

CHAPTER 50

THE ROAD TO NOWHERE

"I looked out to sea while Phridon consoled me, though I could not shake my sorrow. In time, the cool air began to quench the fires in me. I sat next to my friend, leaning against him, and dared to hope a sun might still hide behind the clouds darkening my world. We stayed there long after he finished speaking, and it was me who broke the silence."

"The burden I carry has worn deep ruts in the road of my soul. I was utterly alone until you aided me with news to help my quest. You too have spent your days like me, with no equal in all the men of your Kingdom."

"To be sure, you are unique among those God set on this earth, but I fear a part of me drifts untethered and lost. I must ask for the wisdom of your counsel. How can I return joy to my heart? Without the sun I seek, nothing remains for me. I cannot survive alone without her."

"When I finished, Phridon sat in silence for a long time, thinking. Then he took my hands and knelt before me. He looked up into my face as he spoke. 'You are King and Lord of India and came to my lands as brother and friend. I could not ask more from God than to meet you.'"

"'You must appreciate the bond we share as brothers. No act of gratitude is better than simply being friends. Because of this, I am chained to you as your servant and willingly obey your command. It is my wish to ease your pain, and I will endeavor to aid you.'"

"'Mulghazanzar is a highway for ships through these parts. What happens abroad will be heard here, for all manner of people come to us from far and distant places. If any know of her, we will find them, and in doing so soothe the fire which consumes you.'"

"'Fear not, my friend. We will seek news with a fleet of ships from our ports. I will send experienced men who know the ways of the sea and have visited many foreign regions. They will help you find the moon of your heart. I ask only for your patience, as these things take time.'"

"'Do not allow your hand to grow restless or let your mind torture you while we wait. Together we can hope to find a way for you and her, bringing an end to your grief. Hold your head high, beside me, and we will defeat the evil of Fate with joy.'"

"When he finished speaking, we embraced, and I gave thanks to Heaven for the light he brought to my life. Then, we made our way back to the city with newfound resolve. On our arrival, he called the Captains of every ship to us."

"He ordered them to cross the seas seeking news of Nestan. None were to sit idle. Instead, they must overcome every hardship which came upon them, scouring the waters day and night."

"We sent men to every corner of the world, and I confess my shame in allowing myself to rediscover happiness. The efforts of our search consoled me for a time, and the pain of separation lightened. I found joy, believing I would learn news of her with the help of Phridon."

"While we waited, he commanded a throne to be set up for me in the palace, placing it next to his. He apologized for not showing me the respect I was due as King of India and made himself my subject. Though I protested, he would not relent, and his own soldiers and people swore allegiance to me."

"But what point is there in lengthening the story? Captains came to us from everywhere. They roamed all ports and crossed every sea, yet none had news. With every new ship, the weight around my neck increased. My burden grew from ten to a hundred and then to a thousand. Each day, the river of my sorrow flowed anew and left me rent with grief. Soon, my thoughts darkened, weighing heavily on me."

"I decided it was time to leave and called to my friend to tell him of my intentions. 'With God as my witness, it pains me to speak these words. You are a brother to me. My time with you is a balm to my wounded soul, yet I am unable to go on living like this. My heart falls further from me with each passing moment.'"

"'It crushes me to receive no news of my heart's desire. Time slips from my grasp like sand, and all the joy in this life becomes bitter to me. I am sorry, but I can remain here no longer. The sea brought nothing but sorrow, and I must ask you to release me. I will roam the lands, seeking her abroad. Though I fear the day and night will become one to me without you, if I do not go, I will bring about my own ruin.'"

"Phridon's expression turned from gold to gray as I spoke, his heart lost to grief at learning of my departure. He wished for anything other than what I requested, but he did not try to change my mind when he answered. 'My brother, this news lays heavy on me. These past months with you as my companion have been the best of my life.'"

"'Now I find the sails of my spirit fallen. The winds of Fate blow what I desire most from me. Yet, I will not stop you. How could I call happiness my own if I stole it from another? I give you my leave and blessing, though it wounds me to do so.'"

"How his words pained me. Until meeting him, I had no home in the world other than India. He and the people of his Kingdom had given me something I would never be able to repay. They gave me a measure of peace I did not realize the importance of until it had slipped away from me."

"Their gift was what gave me strength to go on. Where the city of my soul once fell to ruin, their love showed me I could hope for a way out of the rubble. But I could not stay. Although it was difficult, nothing remained but for me to leave the Kingdom of Mulghazanzar."

"With no other choice, we prepared for the journey. Asmath and my two Knights readied themselves, and we made our way towards the gates. The citizens were sad to see us go. Some wept pitifully at our passing, throwing fresh cut roses, and wishing us to return in health and haste. They left us wanting for nothing, save perhaps a less sorrowful departure."

"Phridon surprised me above all, presenting a gift of inestimable value. He gave me the black stallion I ride, and I cherish the words he spoke to this day."

"'Brother, there is no way for me to accompany you, though I know the road will be difficult. In place of me by your side, I give my steed to you. None can catch him, and if you wish, horse and rider can vanish from all pursuers in a moment. May he carry you safely through any troubles which pass while you are away from the safety of our city.'"

"As we left, the sorrow of our parting watered the ground. Most of all, between myself and the brother I was leaving behind. We embraced one last time, kissing one another like brothers. My heart wept as well for Asmath, as I knew she had spent many an evening conversing with Phridon under the stars. They would miss one another, but she and I could have no peace until we rescued Nestan from her captors."

CHAPTER 51

DEATH OF A KNIGHT

"As we left the city, I kept my eyes forward, fearing my heart would stop if I looked over my shoulder at the haven of tranquility behind us. I knew there would be no rest for me until I held the woman I loved in my arms again, but I did not know how to find her. Until now, everything I had tried came to no end. Each time I found a tree, it bore no fruit. My soul lay barren as a forgotten vineyard, with only crows to pick away the bits of sustenance and hope I still clung to."

"The road away from Mulghazanzar wound a seemingly endless path into darkness, but I held to the brotherhood Phridon shared with me and used it to light my way. Fate left me no choice but to seek my love by whatever route remained. I reminded myself God does as he wants, and men and women are at their best when they open their hearts to His will. Since the sea was closed to me, I would roam the wilds."

"We traveled for months, spending our days between the shores and hills, so I might watch both for any sign of Nestan. Yet, I saw nothing of her. Nor did I find any man among those we met who carried news of two black Kadj sorcerers with a woman who shone like a moon. Wherever I turned, only endless forests greeted me. If another way forward existed, it remained hidden."

"Eventually, I decided that wandering in vain was pointless. My time was wasted seeking what Heaven denied me.

For more than two years, I had been searching for my heart's desire but found nothing other than an empty track. Grief consumed me, and I gave myself over to the wilderness which had taken root in my soul. I decided to become like the beasts and live among them. Perhaps their company would help me forget the tide of sorrow I could no longer fight."

"I said as much to Asmath, telling her and my two loyal Knights I was giving up. Though, as my tongue had already given itself over to the way of wild things, my words were short. 'I brought ruin on you all, and you have every reason to speak against the course I chose. I understand this and do not want to see you destroy your lives to no end. Look no more at the endless misery which surrounds my life and follow me no further. Find your own way, lest you break yourselves on mountain of grief I carry.'"

"Yet for all my efforts to discourage their companionship, they would not leave my side. They chastised me for what I said. 'We cannot hear what you say, for the heart we know and love is not the one speaking to us. There is no other we would call Lord or follow. If God did not turn us away from your path, why should you?'"

"Their devotion returned a measure of humanity to me. I remembered how Fate eventually makes a man lost to himself, however valiant he may be. Reminded of this, I did not send my companions away, but my wildness did not fully depart. I could no longer bear the sight of other men and stayed far from the villages and cities we passed, preferring to seek out the haunts of goats and stags. Eventually, we rode over every plain and hill until I found these caves. However, they were not empty."

"Devi had hollowed them out with their arcane skill and made their homes here, but we did not know this. When we entered, the monsters attacked us. Our armor was unbuckled, and their evil magic killed my two faithful Knights. Yet, they could not overcome me so easily. I fought them, fiercely defending myself as I slew one after the other. In the end, I stood once more amidst the carnage of my sword, covered in their blood.

I remembered my past battles, all to no purpose, and became a hundred times more bitter towards the world at the loss of my Knights."

"Since then, I am here. Asmath is my only companion. We hold close to what is left of the sun we lost, yet we are both consumed by fire with our tragedy. She will not abandon me or leave, and I must protect her, so even death is denied to me. We are alike in this, chained to a fate we are unable to escape and forever grasping for a way to free ourselves."

"These days, grief has made a madman of me. I roam the fields with no direction. Sometimes I forget all else in my misery, but nothing changes. I willingly court death, but God refuses my plea. However much I whet my blade with the blood of others, killing myself remains beyond me. Undoubtedly, I will die here in these caves, but I still cling to the dream of finding my love."

"This story is the sum of what you sought from me. I would give you some token to take with you to Tinatin, but I dare not part with the memories these few possessions bring me. I have only her armlet, which you have already seen, and this panther skin, which reminds me of her grace and beauty. I keep them with me wherever I go. Aside from these things, I fear she is a flower long since faded except to our memory."

When the last words left his lips, Tariel moaned in pain as tears streamed from his eyes. His cheeks turned from ruby rose to pale amber. Forceful sobs shattered his form, and he shook uncontrollably. Avtandil and Asmath cried as well, water dripping from their eyelashes like rain from the tailfeathers of a raven. They tried to calm their friend, holding and soothing him, but it took many hours before he could speak again.

CHAPTER 52

OATHS AND PROMISES

After he calmed himself, Tariel sat quietly for almost an hour before speaking to Avtandil again.

"You must leave now. The time for you to meet Tinatin is nearly past. If you do not return, she will think you are lost and weep bitterly. Do not add this to my burden. Go to your sun, for I made your way the best I can in sharing my tale, though I took no pleasure in doing so. I will manage myself as God sees fit. Perhaps, if my prayers are heard, I will die."

Considering the weight of the dark words his friend spoke, Avtandil took him by the hands, looking at him intently before responding.

"In truth, I do not know how I will leave you here. When I think of home, tears spring to my eyes. I cannot imagine any road I might take which would not lead back to you, for who can forsake his own brother? Yet I must say more than this, though it may be unpleasant to your ears."

"Your talk of dying is foolish. It cuts into the soul of Asmath, and it will not bring comfort to the rose of your heart. How will she survive without you? Who else will save her? To die is to do nothing. Death is the final accomplishment of the lowest creature in the world. Would you make her a gift of your failure?"

"All your life, you have done what no one else could, but now, where have your power and faith departed to? What sort of hero turns back from the last steps of his journey? You love Nestan with fires more intense than any sun, so I say it is time for you to live. Stop looking to death, for it is the easy way out. Living is the most difficult thing any man can do for another."

"What physician does not call on another doctor to aid him when he is ill, however renowned his skill? This is true of everything in life, for one person often knows what is better for the other. I am no different in this with my care for you. Where before only Asmath advised you, now I am here too. My heart bleeds no less than yours, and this lets me understand you like no other."

"You must listen now, not once, or ten times, but rather a hundred. Keep my words in your mind until they become a litany to you, for you cannot do well for yourself like this. Trust me, and we will overcome this tragedy together. I will not abandon you or lightly depart, however heartsick you may be."

"Like me, you are a Knight. You came into the world as a warrior, and it is how you will die. But men like us are measured by the sum of their words and actions, which is why I need your solemn vow to remain here until I return. If you promise this, I will never forsake you. My place will be by your side, and God willing, we will find your rose together. Assure me of this, or I can never leave."

Tariel held tighter to his friend's hands, his voice shaking with emotion as he responded.

"I do not understand how you came to care so deeply for me, but your departure is also difficult for me. Still, I find hope for my love and myself in you, for you are like a nightingale to a rose. Though I am wilted and faded, still you remain by my side. Do not imagine I could forget you, whatever may happen. You will be on my mind every day, and I will pray to see you again before my life is spent."

"When you return, the sadness of your absence will dissolve, and I will rejoice. I will not flee into the fields, for when I am in your presence, my sorrow is gone like a bird on the wind."

Then the two Knights promised neither would forget the

other in time of need. They cut their hands, binding their oath in blood, and swearing before God on all they loved. Avtandil swore to come back before the end of the next season, and Tariel agreed to wait for him.

They sat together the rest of the night, sharing stories and wisdom with one another until the sky lightened. Though he wished to linger, Avtandil had more than one vow to keep. His parting words were short and choked with emotion.

"I must go now to my own sun, but I will not forsake you. I will tell her your story and confirm her love of me. When this is done, I will be back, and whether it takes one year or a hundred, we will roam the earth together until we find her. Wherever she may be, or whoever holds her, none will stand against us."

Separated by the necessity of their obligations, they kissed the cheeks of one another and turned away. Each carrying his own sorrow as the other left. Tariel returned to the cave, and Avtandil prepared to ride out.

Asmath came to the edge of the clearing as he readied himself to leave, weeping as she knelt before him. Lacing her fingers together, she begged a promise from him to come back soon or see her faded like a violet. He turned at her words, reaching out and grasping her hands in his.

"I will think of nothing in the space of my absence other than the two of you. Before the next season finishes, I will return. In this time, do not let him wander elsewhere, and do not fear I will abandon my vows. If I have not returned before then, be sure a great malady has befallen me."

Then he kissed her on the forehead and mounted his horse, tears cascading down his cheeks as he rode away. Once more, he crossed through the rushes and into the plains beyond. Though the road home was long, this time, he traveled with a clear purpose. He would share news of the Knight in the Panther Skin with Tinatin and then return to the caves. Together he and Tariel would find Nestan or die in the attempt.

AN END TO THE BEGINNING

THE TALE CONTINUES

Looking down at the empty cups and bottles on my table, I wondered why he stopped. I asked what became of Avtandil and Tariel but received no answer. When I lifted my eyes, I realized the man was gone. At first, I thought he might have stepped away, but the waitress told me I had been sitting alone all evening.

Confused, I looked in my journal and saw it was full. While what I had written could have been found at the bottom of a wine bottle, it certainly hadn't originated there. Looking through my notes, I could see most of the tale, but it was incomplete. I needed to know what happened next, though I had no idea how to find the man again.

Then I noticed a paragraph in Georgian on the front of my notebook, which I soon learned was a name and a clue.

"The tears and joy of the Georgian people are written into The Knight in the Panther Skin. Each of us finds our soul and heart in the pages of this great work, and we draw our best feelings, intentions, and thoughts from it." - Ilia Chavchavadze

This text was a key I would use to unlock more of the story. In the morning, I resolved to learn who Ilia was, and the history of this country which had so captivated my heart and imagination. The tale I had come to love was far from finished, and neither was I. After all, good stories are no different than fine wine. They are not easy to find, and however good they are, there's an end in every book and a bottom to every bottle. I just hadn't reached the end of this one yet.

ABOUT THE AUTHORS

H. J. BUELL

H. J. Buell is a native of Virginia who grew up between the majesty of the Blue Ridge Mountains and the complex history of Washington, DC, and its secret societies. He left home early and eventually traveled the world, working with different people and learning their beliefs, customs, and histories.

Over time he found himself drawn into wars, where he worked with governments, NGOs, and various intelligence agencies. The more he worked, the less he found to believe in from the systems he had been raised to champion. Looking for a better way, he stumbled into Georgia, where he would spill out the joys and tragedies of his experiences through writing.

Along the way he was introduced to Shota Rustaveli's epic poem, The Knight in the Panther Skin. The story captured his imagination, and he spent the next three years rewriting it as a series of three English novels. Avtandil's Quest is the first of these novels. His hope is for the story to rekindle the hearts and minds of people who aspire to make themselves into better people, and in doing so, sow the seeds of a better world.

ANA GABUNIA

Ana Gabunia was born and raised in Kutaisi, during the darkest times of modern Georgia. She studied French by candlelight and read stories with her family. It was there, in the flickering light of a single flame, where the dreams of a little girl began to grow into something more.

In her dreams, men and women fought together to make the world a better place, much like what she had read in the oldest Georgian tales. She held onto those dreams and traveled abroad after graduating. Her career paths led her through the fields of diplomacy, human rights, and journalism, yet she never found what she was looking for.

The truths she sought were not in New York or Paris, and eventually her travels led her back home to Kutaisi. Once home, she rediscovered the beauty and truth of The Knight in the Panther Skin. Viewing the story through the eyes of an adult, she decided to bring the text into the modern world where others could appreciate the depth of its beauty and philosophy.

Her hand was instrumental in the creation of Avtandil's Quest and the other two books in the trilogy. Currently she's translating the English version into Georgian and assisting with translations in other languages. With time, she hopes to see copies of her books available in every language.

We hope you enjoyed reading Avtandil's Quest.
If you'd like to learn more about us,
please visit our website!

https://hjbuell.com